To Love Again

Mission Point Press

Published by Mission Point Press
MissionPointPress.com

978-1-968761-15-8
LoC: Available upon request
Printed in the United States of America

To Love Again

Anne Edmondson Barbour

Sixth in the Love Connections Series

M·P·P

www.MissionPointPress.com

One

Mattie Wilson was getting dressed for church, at the same time, thinking about the wedding she had attended the day before. It was a wonderful, happy occasion for Mark Thomas and Austen Wiley.

He was the owner of TrailWays and she had come from Overland Park, Kansas, to work there for the season. As someone said, he had not expected a woman, nor had he expected love. Though anyone in their presence could see it, even feel it, the two tried to ignore it. When they finally accepted and admitted their love for each other, Kate Pearson said, "It's about time," and everyone else echoed it.

Josh, Mattie's son, and Mark had been friends since high school, and though he was a teacher, in the summers, he worked at TrailWays. When it looked like Mark was going to let Austen go back to Kansas, Josh convinced him he would regret it forever.

Josh had told his mother that a friend from out of town was coming for the wedding and would be staying with him, but there was no opportunity to meet whoever he was. Maybe they would be at church. There, she made her way to the area where she usually sat.

Sometimes Anita O'Neill joined her, but looking around, Mattie didn't see her.

She smiled at her thought that Anita would be a good match for Josh. He had no girlfriend, and in Mattie's mind, it was time for him to marry and produce some grandchildren for her. Somehow, it had escaped her notice that Josh never sat with her when Anita did.

~

Mattie often went to Eddie's Café for lunch after church, but not today. While sitting in the worship center, thinking again about yesterday's event, her mind had drifted back to her wedding. What a happy, wonderful day that was. But sadness also washed over her, as she felt anew the loss of Andrew, that wonderful man she had loved so much. Thankfully, that didn't happen often.

That feeling was still with her as she pulled into her driveway. The first thing she did when she entered the house was go to Andrew's picture. She picked it up and held it as she sat in a nearby chair.

Oh, Andrew. I am missing you so much today. I went to a wedding yesterday, and I have been remembering that special day when we got married. I loved you so much, had loved you so long. I could hardly believe you loved me, but there was never a question in those years we had together.

There were tears as she placed the picture where it always rested.

I'll call Nancy. Talking to her will cheer me up.

"Hello, Mom."

"Hello. I was hoping I wouldn't have to leave a message. I wanted to hear your voice. How was your training yesterday? Sure wish you could have come to the wedding."

"I'm always glad to hear your voice too. And I wish I could have gone to the wedding, but the class demonstrating new therapy techniques was very enlightening; I was glad to be there. Even had the opportunity to practice some of them. I'm sure there will be occasions when patients will benefit," her daughter told her.

"How was the wedding? Who were the attendants? Was Josh one?"

"No, he wasn't. They only had Austen's little boy, David, as ringbearer and Mark's niece, Patsy, as flower girl. You probably remember she is Matt's daughter. Josh was there, of course."

"Did he have a date, or was he alone, as always?"

"No date, though he was dancing with a beautiful young woman I hadn't seen before. She caught the bridal bouquet and was holding it while they danced. Kate Pearson came to take it; maybe she's a relative of Kate or Bill. Or maybe someone who visited TrailWays and got acquainted with all of them.

"He told me a few days ago that a friend from out of town was coming for the wedding and would stay with him."

Nancy wondered if she might know who her brother's friend was and said, "You hadn't mentioned that, who was it?"

"I don't know; Josh didn't say, and he didn't introduce us at the wedding. Actually, the only person I saw with him was the woman he was dancing with."

"That's interesting. From what you've told me, I'm guessing he wasn't at church?"

"He wasn't. I figured his company hadn't left yet."

Nancy noted some sadness in her mother's voice and asked, "Did you have lunch at Eddie's?"

"No, just came on home. Actually, thought I should have found out more about Josh's plans and invited them for lunch. And you, too. It's been awhile since we all had lunch together."

"You're right. Maybe we can plan that for next Sunday. I could even drive in and go to church with you."

"That sounds good. I'm so glad we had this talk. Love you."

"Love you, too, Mom."

Mattie felt better after her talk with Nancy and thought about calling her son, still curious about his friend and the young woman, but told herself, *Martha Elizabeth Yates Wilson, he's an adult man entitled to some privacy with no need to tell you his business.*

⌁

Jefferson Tate missed seeing his daughter, Jerilyn, at church. She had her own home, but she usually sat with him on Sunday mornings. She had left Friday, flying to Nebraska for the wedding of her friend, Austen. She would be returning home tomorrow.

His sons, Jack and Jon, still lived with him but weren't always able to attend church. They were in careers with shifts that meant they were often on duty on Sundays.

It had been several years since his wife's death, but there were still times the grief returned, as it had this Sunday morning when he was sitting alone in church. Jeff was unsure what triggered the emotion, perhaps thinking of the wedding of Jerilyn's friend and remembering his and the years he and Joyce were together—happy years.

After church, he was in his vehicle—an SUV much like those used by the police department—considering whether to go home and fix his own lunch or go to a restaurant. He thought of Cinzetti's, Jack Stack Barbecue, or maybe Dragon Inn. It would be lonely at home, but in some ways, eating alone at a restaurant was worse. At least there would be others around, creating the clamor that comes from people conversing, ordering, and enjoying their meals.

Jeff hadn't been to Cinzetti's recently and decided to go there. No need to look at a menu, trying to decide what he might like. It had a wonderful buffet and he could see the dishes and choose what he preferred. It was a favorite place for many, and he might even see people from church.

He was filling his plate when he heard, "Hey LT."

It had to be someone he had served with on the PD. Jeff didn't know of any others who shortened Lieutenant to LT. When he turned toward the man, he was surprised to see John Kelley. They'd not only served together several years, but had been good friends. Then John moved to another state and another department; and as close as they had been, over a period of time, they'd lost touch.

"Kelley, what a surprise. Good to see you. Have you moved back to Overland Park?"

He was pretty much finished with his selections, as Jeff was, and the men almost juggled their plates as they shook hands.

"No. Where are you sitting? I'll join you." Kelley motioned to the waitress, letting her know of the change.

Once they were settled, Kelley said, "You asked if I've moved back to OP. One of Shirley's friends was planning a fiftieth birthday party. She wanted to come, so we decided to take a driving vacation, seeing some of the country on the way here.

"The party is this afternoon. I wasn't invited," he said with a grin. "Needed to find someplace for lunch. Someone told me about Cinzetti's, so I decided to try it. Drove around OP on the way. Sure has grown since we left."

"Yes, it has; sometimes hard for me to realize how much it has changed. Are you still policing?"

"No," Kelley told him. "I was unlucky enough to be involved in a bad accident. So guess you could say I was medically retired.

"What about you? And how is your wife and family?"

Jeff said, "I'm retired too." After a brief hesitation, he continued, "Joyce died four years ago."

"Oh, I'm sorry to hear that. She was a special lady."

"Yes."

"What about your kids? Probably married and maybe you're Grandpa Tate?"

Kelley was looking down and missed the sad look on Jeff's face.

"No, none married and don't even have a special someone, so no grandkids. But I'm ready to have some running around.

"Jerilyn, my daughter, has her own place and is a teacher. Jack and Jon are still living with me. Jon is a firefighter and Jack is at the Police Academy."

"Police Academy; so the legacy continues?"

"Yeah. I tried not to be disappointed when he started out as a newspaper man, kind of following in his mother's footsteps. It didn't take long for him to know that wasn't for him. He said law enforcement was calling, though he did try to ignore it for a while.

"What about your kids?"

"Don't know if you remember, we have two sons, Mike and Terry? Mike is studying and working to becoming a doctor. Terry's still deciding but seems to be leaning toward law—the civilian, lawyer side. Says he wants to be a DA."

"How do you feel about that?" Jeff asked.

John told him, "It's okay; main thing is for them to be happy and satisfied with their choice."

~

When they were leaving Cinzetti's, Jeff said, "This has been great. Let's don't lose touch again."

The two exchanged addresses and phone numbers and hugged before heading to their cars.

Two

attie was anxious to talk to her son but waited until Monday. Expecting that he had been at school where he was a teacher, it was late afternoon when she called.

"Hi, Mom."

"Hello, Josh. How was your day after the busy weekend? Sorry I didn't get to visit with you at the wedding and meet your guest."

Hoping she would have no more words about the weekend, he answered only, "It was Monday. How about yours?"

In fact, he had taken the day off from teaching to take his guest to the airport.

"Oh, nothing special; but then that's usual. Nancy and I talked after church yesterday. I told her I was sorry I hadn't invited you and your friend for lunch."

There was a pause as if each considered whether to say more. Josh was remembering that he was glad his mother wasn't at Eddie's Café when he and Jerilyn went there Sunday for a late lunch.

Jerilyn … He had been so glad she came for the wedding. How he wished she could have stayed longer. Why had he avoided introducing her to his mother? And why hadn't he kissed her, even when he took her to the airport this morning? It wasn't as if he didn't want to.

"Josh?"

"Oh, sorry. We had lunch. I didn't expect you to provide it. Maybe next time." Hoping there would be a next time.

Mattie repeated, "Maybe next time.

"When we were talking, your sister and I realized it's been awhile since the three of us had lunch together. Maybe we can do that next Sunday? Nancy said she could drive to Plattsford and go to church with us too. Would you be able to join us?"

"Yeah," Josh said. "I don't talk to my sister enough—you either. How about I pick you up?"

Josh knew that Anita O'Neill made a point of sitting with his mother at church. If he and she walked in together, that couldn't happen. He was still puzzled that she had even walked into his house when Jerilyn was there. How had that happened, and why? Whether his mother knew or not, Anita did, that his guest was a young woman.

"Oh, that would be wonderful." Then changing the subject, Mattie asked, "How is school? How many students do you have?"

~

Jeff wondered how Jerilyn's trip went. She had shared very little about the one she had taken in August to see her friend Austen. At the time, there'd been no expectation of a wedding. But his daughter hadn't seemed surprised when she learned there would be. She mentioned a friend of Mark's she had met and seemed glad that she would see him again.

As far as Jeff knew, Jerilyn didn't have a boyfriend, but he wasn't sure how a long-distance courtship might work. As it often did, his thoughts turned to Joyce; they could see each other anytime they wanted without any effort.

As he was pondering those days and how special they were, Jerilyn called.

"Hi, Dad. Wanted to let you know I'm home."

"Glad you did," Jeff said. "I was wondering. How was everything?"

"Wonderful. Austen is so happy; and Mark obviously adores her."

"Did you get to spend time with Mark's friend—Josh?"

Jerilyn hadn't told her dad that she would be staying with Josh and still chose not to mention it—maybe later. After all, they hadn't even kissed.

"Yes."

"And?"

"And, what?"

"How are you feeling about him?" Jeff asked. "I got the impression that you felt more than just friendship."

Jerilyn said, "You're right. I should have known you would sense that. I do like him—a lot. And I think he feels the same about me. But there's a lot of miles between us."

Jeff said, "I can certainly see how that could present a challenge."

Wanting to change the subject, Jerilyn asked, "Anything new with you?"

"Well, actually nothing new, but I did run into an old friend at Cinzetti's yesterday. You were out of town and both boys were at work, so I went out to eat after church.

"Do you remember the Kelleys?" Jeff asked. "John was a special friend, then he got a job with another PD in California and we eventually lost touch."

Jerilyn said, "Not sure; the name is familiar. So was he the friend you saw?"

"Yes. His wife was at a birthday party. He needed to go someplace for lunch and somebody told him about Cinzetti's.

"So serendipitous, but we had a good visit, shared what's happening with our kids," her dad told her.

"I'm glad. Now I need to make sure I'm ready for school tomorrow," Jerilyn said. "Love you, Dad."

"Love you, too."

~

Mattie had finished her breakfast but took her cup of coffee with her and headed for the front porch. She made herself comfortable in one of the chairs and began to survey her flower beds. It was autumn, time to prepare them for the winter and determine whether there might be bare spots needing some fall color.

She would be driving to Plattsford to get groceries, and might drive by the nursery, see what they have, maybe find something new.

Growing flowers had been a special love for Mattie since that had been one of her projects in 4-H. For that, there had been only one small bed, and that remained the norm until Andrew died. Sadly, she'd had to sell the ranch; that was when she and her children moved to town. Their first spring here, she dug up a spot for one small bed. It was a few years later that she started expanding and adding.

As she did so, she had butterflies and pollinators in mind, wanting to plant things that attracted them. She would be able to enjoy watching them and know she was helping the environment. Thus, many of them were wildflowers.

She was sorry Nancy had never been interested in that activity. With the thought that Josh and Anita O'Neill might marry someday, she wondered whether growing flowers might interest her.

Setting that notion aside and taking another look at the beds, Mattie wondered if it might be time to start reducing their size, perhaps even fill some of them in. Maybe next year.

~

Jeff finished his breakfast, straightened up the kitchen, then poured a cup of coffee and carried it out to the deck. He wanted to take advantage of the warm sunny morning. It was well into the fall season, and he knew these days wouldn't last.

He looked around the backyard, taking special note of the spots where Joyce's flower beds had once provided so much color and attracted butterflies and bees. They had been so important to her; she had even loved the digging and weeding, along with the planting, that resulted in so much beauty.

Now he felt regret. *I'm sorry, Joyce, that I haven't cared for them, that they have been so neglected.*

Jeff remembered the time when they were walking around together as she was cutting flowers for a bouquet. He had told her, "If anything ever happens to you, they'll probably all just die. I don't have a clue of how to take care of them."

Joyce had put the bouquet down, reached her arms around him for a hug, and said, "It'll be okay if you just remember. I wouldn't expect you to take care of them."

Oh, Joyce. I do remember. And how I wish you were still here to take care of them.

~

Before Mattie went to the store, she planned her menu for Sunday's lunch, then checked the cabinets to determine what she had and what she needed.

By the time she finished her shopping, Mattie decided not to go to the nursery. Instead, since it was lunchtime, she stopped at Eddie's to pick up something. While she waited, a woman who had paid and was ready to leave stopped where she was sitting.

"Oh, Mattie, how are you? Missed seeing you here Sunday. I had things to do after church but came here for a late lunch."

"I'm fine. Was feeling a bit downcast after service, so went on home," Mattie told her.

The woman said, "I did notice Josh was here with a young woman."

"Oh?"

Just then, Mattie's name was called, indicating her takeout was ready. When she went to the counter, the other woman left.

On her way home, Mattie pondered what the woman had said about seeing Josh on Sunday. If it truly was her son, who might the young woman have been. Forgetting about seeing Josh dancing at the wedding, she wondered if it might have been Anita. Perhaps she would invite Anita to the lunch planned for Sunday, having no idea how Josh felt about the woman.

Three

In the days and weeks since she had returned from the wedding, Jeff watched as Jerilyn went from a radiance of happiness to almost gloom. He didn't know whether to question her or comment on it. He hoped she was at least confiding in her Covenant Group.

But she wasn't. At first, there were texts and phone calls between her and Josh, but they had tapered off. Jerilyn wasn't sure of the reason, but on those days she was overwhelmingly blue, she would scroll to some of the texts she had received from him, reading them again. Though she and Josh had established a special friendship, she remembered Anita O'Neill, who obviously wanted a relationship with him. Maybe that had happened.

That memory was enhanced when an email from Austen mentioned seeing the two together often. If they were indeed becoming a couple, she didn't want to do anything that would hinder Josh's chance for happiness.

~

Thanksgiving came and, as in the past several years, Jerilyn prepared the meal with her father, Jeff, and brothers, Jack and Jon, joining her for the day. Even they noticed how her demeanor had changed, Jack especially noticing she had lost that glow she had worn for a few weeks after her trip to Nebraska for the wedding of her friend.

～

In Nebraska, Mattie prepared Thanksgiving dinner for her, Josh, and Nancy. They also celebrated Nancy's birthday; occasionally it was on the same day. Even when it wasn't, there were always candles on the pumpkin birthday pie.

Nancy made note of how Josh had become almost morose, so completely different than that Sunday several weeks ago. She chose not to ask about what might have caused the difference, thinking instead, *I'll call him later. Don't talk to my brother often enough anyway.*

If Mattie detected any difference, she attributed it to his reacting to the happiness of his friend Mark and her son not having that special one. *I need to find a way to get him and Anita together. They would be such a sweet couple.*

～

Thing was, just as Jerilyn in Kansas was missing the communication between them, so was Josh. And as she turned often to the texts from him, he scrolled to the ones from her to read again.

Adding to that gloom, one day, when he was visiting at Trail-Ways, Austen mentioned getting an email from one of her church friends in Kansas about Jerilyn and a new teacher at her school. That knowledge underscored Josh's determination not to contact Jerilyn. He cared so much for her, he didn't want to create a situation that

15

might generate dissatisfaction. How could he have this strong feeling when he and Jerilyn had not even kissed?

~

Time passed, the special season of Christmas, as well as the months early in the new year, and spring had arrived. Mattie received catalogs loaded with pictures of flowers, plants, and trees in the mail from a couple of nurseries. In the fall, she had thought about downsizing her flower beds, but the images called to her, tempting her much as a catalog full of toys affects a child.

It would be several weeks before new plants could be added, and there was cleanup that needed to be done. Mattie could start on that when weather allowed; and while she was doing that, she could decide about adding anything new.

In Overland Park, Kansas, Jonson Tate came home at the end of his shift to see Jeff with a spade and a rake, staring at an area in the backyard which was kind of ragged looking.

"Hey, Dad, what's happening?"

"Nothing yet," Jeff said. "Just been thinking about rejuvenating a couple of your mom's flower beds. There's still evidence of them after all this time. But I don't really have a clue."

Jon noticed tears in his dad's eyes, knowing he was missing Joyce, then said, "I sure don't know. Maybe you could check at Family Tree Nursery. I remember going there with Mom a few times. They have everything, even fish."

At the word *fish*, Jeff surreptitiously wiped his eyes and asked, "Fish?"

"Yeah, you know for fishponds."

Jeff moved close to his son and hugged him. "Thanks, Son. Good idea."

He gathered the tools, and the men walked back to the house talking about the flower beds and how they had enjoyed them while Joyce had done all the work.

~

While their parents were considering what to do about their flower beds, both Josh and Jerilyn continued in their despondency. Of all their family and friends, only Mark had an idea of the true situation, especially with Josh, who seemed to be losing interest in everything. Though he did occasionally ask Mark if Austen ever heard anything from Jerilyn.

Mark and Austen were planning a trip to Overland Park to visit her parents and former in-laws. While there, they would go through the storage shed where she had put her things before leaving for Nebraska. They would rent a truck to carry whatever she decided to keep back to TrailWays.

Schools would soon be on spring break. Mark knew Josh was always ready to be of assistance, so they chose those days for their trip. The fact that Austen was pregnant provided a good reason to ask for Josh's help.

Josh was pleased to give a hand and would become the second driver on the trip back to Nebraska, freeing Austen to spend a few days more with her family before flying home. At the same time, it was in his mind he might even see Jerilyn.

~

Jefferson Tate wasn't sure what to think when Jerilyn called to see if he was home. She had told him earlier that Austen was coming to Overland Park to get her things in storage. His daughter was going to drive to the Morgans', Austen's parents, to see her.

Then she called to learn whether he was home and to tell him she would be stopping by and was bringing a visitor. Jeff wondered who the visitor might be but was always glad to have company and met them at the door.

Jerilyn introduced them, "Josh Wilson, this is my dad, Jefferson Tate, though everyone knows him as Jeff."

As they shook hands, Jeff recalled that his daughter had said little about her trip to visit Austen and then a few weeks later for her wedding. She had said even less about Josh, but he remembered the lilt in her voice when she mentioned him.

The two men were impressed with each other and Jeff thought of Josh as a potential son-in-law while Josh wondered if he might be meeting his future father-in-law.

Josh didn't meet her brothers, but he said, "Maybe next time."

He used those words several times to Jerilyn during his short visit, glad they had this time together. But perhaps, most importantly, they each learned there was no one else for the other, and finally, there was a kiss.

~

Mattie knew nothing of the love Josh felt for a girl in Kansas. So when Anita O'Neill contacted her, seemingly concerned she couldn't get in touch with him, his mother happily encouraged her, letting her know where he was. Though Mattie had hopes they would become a couple, as did Anita, she hadn't grasped that Anita had no special feelings for her. And certainly, Josh had no special feelings for Anita.

Josh knew he needed to tell his mother about Jerilyn sooner, rather than later. So when he and Mark pulled into TrailWays, he called her.

"Hi Mom, we're back, tired. I'll probably come back tomorrow to help move things out of the truck. But I need to see you, tell you about Jerilyn. How about I stop by early in the morning?"

"I'm so glad you're home safely, and I'm always glad to see you whatever time. How about coming for breakfast—seven o'clock?"

Just as Josh's call to his mother ended, Jerilyn called. He told her, "Having breakfast with my mom tomorrow, going to tell her about you. Should have a long time ago. Guess I wanted you to be my secret love."

When Josh arrived at his mother's, she told him, "I don't see you enough, feel like I'm missing out on things happening in your life."

After setting a filled plate in front of him and taking a seat herself, Mattie asked, "Okay, who is Jerilyn?"

"Jerilyn is a friend of Austen's."

His mother noticed the way he said *Jerilyn'* was like an endearment.

Josh continued, "I met her when she and another friend drove to TrailWays last summer to visit Austen. Though it was only a few days, it was enough for me to know I wanted her to be a special part of my life.

"And she's the friend who came for the wedding and stayed with me. I know I should have introduced you; maybe I was afraid of exposing my feelings."

"If she's a friend of Austen's, does that mean she lives in Kansas?"

"Yeah, a long way," Josh answered. "But I did get to spend time with her when I was there helping Mark. Even met her dad."

~

There was so much more Josh needed to tell Mattie and so much more she wanted to know, but he received a text from Mark letting him know he was ready to unload the truck.

~

Josh's mother and Jerilyn's dad were happy their children had found love, but they were still those many miles apart. How could they nourish it? Phone calls, texts, and emails could only do so much.

Then came the Memorial Day holiday weekend, and Josh wanting so much to be able to touch and hold and kiss Jerilyn, he surprised her by flying to Kansas City on Saturday morning. Though Jerilyn already had plans to visit him in a few weeks, he didn't want to wait that long.

Four

Before the trip, Josh had called Jeff and told him his plans to surprise Jerilyn, hoping her dad could ensure she would be home. The three sat together at church the next day, and afterward, Jerilyn invited her dad to come to her house for coffee.

They were enjoying the coffee along with cookies when Josh told Jerilyn he needed some time with her dad. She wondered why but left them alone in the kitchen.

Later, Josh and Jerilyn drove to the Arboretum and Botanical Gardens where they followed the trails and nature walks and enjoyed the environment and ambience. He noticed a bench, led her to it, and said, "Let's rest for a while," then moved to his knee, took her hand, and proposed.

That had been his intention since his decision to make the trip. Though her dad knew about it, when the two returned to Jerilyn's home, she called him to let him know she had accepted.

Josh called his mother to tell her he had proposed to Jerilyn and she had said, "Yes."

He had told her before the trip how important Jerilyn was to him, but she was surprised, thinking it would be longer before he considered marriage. Though she did add, "Even if you are getting older."

Josh and Jerilyn were both sad when he had to leave Monday afternoon. Knowing they would be together again in a couple of weeks lessened that sadness a bit. And now, they could also look forward to the time they would be together for always with no more separations.

Still, after watching Josh drive off, Jerilyn didn't want to be by herself, so she called her dad to see if she could stop by there.

"I'm always glad to see you," Jeff told her. "Come on by."

He had sensed her despondency with Josh's departure and wrapped her in his arms for support as soon as she stepped through the door. She told him how it was getting harder being apart from him.

"When I'm there, we'll need to be making decisions about our future—when we'll get married, where we will live. And that will mean separation from our family for one of us."

"Yes, you two will have to make the decision. No one else should be involved. But if you end up in Nebraska, it will be a new place for me to visit."

School was still in session in Plattsford, Nebraska, so Josh had to be there on Tuesday but went to see his mother at the end of the day. He told Mattie how much he loved Jerilyn. "And I want you to love each other. When she's here, we'll be making plans for our wedding and where we'll live."

～

When Jerilyn arrived, Josh took her to meet his mother before driving to his house. When they were introduced, Mattie held

Jerilyn's hand, then also took Josh's hand. She told her, "I can't say Josh has said much about you, only that he loves you, and that's enough for me."

Before they left, Mattie told her son, "While your special lady is here, I hope you'll give me time to really get acquainted with her."

They kept busy the days Jerilyn was there. She met Josh's sister, Nancy, and her boyfriend, Mitchell Robbins, and visited the ranch he ran with his parents. They got their rings at a store in Scottsbluff, visited TrailWays, and even checked at the schools for a possible opening for a teacher.

~

But when Jerilyn returned home, there was still no date for the wedding. The only sure things settled were that the wedding would be in Overland Park, and they would live in Plattsford, leaving much to think about and much to do, with the tasks mostly falling on her.

The first was to check for available dates at church. In Plattsford, school starts for teachers the last week in August, and it was already mid-July. The wedding was added to the calendar for the second Saturday of August, along with the Friday night preceding for the rehearsal.

Jerilyn would wear her mother's wedding gown, which had hung in the closet of her parent's bedroom for more than thirty years. Many emotions were elicited for both Jerilyn and her dad the day she picked it up.

For her, memories rushed back of the day her mother had showed it to her so many years ago. Jerilyn held the gown, still on its hanger, and pictured her mother's smile as she recalled her wedding day. There was no question Joyce was as much in love with Jeff as the day they married. Jerilyn had regrets that she hadn't visited her mother more, and now she would be separated from her dad.

Tears came to Jeff's eyes, remembering that special day, the day he married Joyce. He was so much in love with his beautiful bride, and that endured all the years of their marriage. He still missed her so much.

He took the gown from Jerilyn, placed it on the bed, then gathered her into his arms. They hugged, comforting each other, remembering those earlier days. At the same time, they were looking forward to new memories that would be made.

With the help of her friends, preparations for the wedding were completed. But Josh and Jerilyn still hadn't decided on attendants. They had discussed possibilities earlier. At another time, Josh would have asked Mark, and Jerilyn would have asked Austen. But they were busy with end-of-season activities at TrailWays, plus Austen was pregnant. To most people, it would probably be considered unusual, but they chose to ask their parents.

Josh said, "The next question is, who will do the asking? Do I ask Mom and you ask your dad? Or the other way around?"

"How about you ask Dad?" Jerilyn asked. "You can tell him about your suit and talk about what he might wear. So that leaves me to call your mother. What do you think?"

"Sounds good to me. When?"

"Let's do it tomorrow."

Jeff answered his phone, "Hello."

"Hi. It's Josh. I'm calling about the wedding."

"Yes. What can I help you with?"

"Jerilyn and I have discussed who to have for our attendants."

Jeff thought perhaps Josh wanted to speak to one of his sons and needed a phone number.

"No," Josh told him. "We thought if you two agreed, we would have our parents. And, yes, we realize many people might consider that unusual.

"So I'm asking you. Will you serve as my best man?"

Jeff told him, "I will be honored."

~

In Plattsford, Mattie answered her phone, "Good morning."

"To you too," Jerilyn answered. "I have a request and hope you won't find it too unusual."

"You have whetted my curiosity," Mattie told her.

After a short pause, Jerilyn asked, "Will you be my matron of honor?"

Mattie had questions but mostly wanted to know who the best man would be. When she learned it would be Jeff, Jerilyn's father, she said, "Yes."

After asking about the colors in the wedding bouquet, she was sure she had the perfect dress.

~

Time moved on, sometimes seeming to rush, then inching along, depending on the person and what needed to be accomplished. Jerilyn and Josh talked every day, so when he sensed she was feeling overwhelmed, he offered to come a week before the wedding, if only to give her moral support. Since Nancy and Mitchell would be attending, they could escort Mattie.

Finally, it was the night of the rehearsal. Jerilyn had picked Josh up at her dad's. Jack and Jon and their ladies, Jayden and Linda, were already at the church, and Jeff was right behind them. Pastor Bradley and his wife, Doris, greeted each of them as they walked into the worship center.

Everyone was there except Mattie, Nancy, and Mitch. Jerilyn wondered if they had got lost on the way. Josh assured her they had driven to the church the day before and knew where it was.

Jeff knew that Josh's mother was to be his daughter's matron of honor but had spent no time considering what she might be like. Now, with these minutes they were waiting, he did wonder—would she look anything like her son? Would she be friendly, outgoing, or maybe shy and retiring?

It didn't really matter. Jeff didn't expect to see her again unless he was visiting Jerilyn someday.

For Mattie, it was much the same. Though she was glad the best man was in her age group.

As soon as the three entered the room, Josh and Jerilyn met them. Josh took his mother's hand and led her to where Jeff was standing to introduce them. Jeff's back was to him, so Josh touched him on the shoulder. When Jeff turned, his eyes went to the woman with Josh and hers to him.

"Jeff, this is my mother, Martha Wilson, though most people call her Mattie."

"Mom, this is Jerilyn's dad, Jefferson Tate, usually known as Jeff."

There were smiles from them both as they reached their hands to the other.

"So glad to meet you," Jeff said. "But you look more like Martie to me, not old enough to be Mattie."

"And I'm happy to meet you, Jefferson."

Grinning at each other, and Jefferson still holding her hand, he led Martie to a seat near the front where the young couples were sitting.

Josh and Jerilyn couldn't miss their parents' reaction to each other and shook their heads, wondering.

Josh gave a nod to Pastor Bradley, indicating everyone was there. He stood and walked to the front, saying, "Let's offer a prayer for this special time.

"Father, we ask Your blessing on Josh and Jerilyn as they begin their life together. Thank You for all the special ones who are celebrating with them."

Then, "Will the bride and groom and any attendants join me? We'll go over some things, then practice for the ceremony."

All the young people had wondered if there were going to be attendants, each knowing they hadn't been asked.

Jeff and Martie waited until Josh and Jerilyn were standing with the pastor, then grinning at each other as if they knew a secret, went to join them. It was unexpected that the parents would fill those positions, but there was a positive response from the others as they all applauded. They all wondered what the reaction might be from guests at the wedding.

Though neither had expected it, there seemed to be a special attraction between Jeff and Martie—as he continued to call her. They enjoyed dancing at the reception, perhaps as much for the opportunity to be in each other's arms as the dance. A few of Jeff's friends were guests at the wedding, and he made a point of introducing Martie.

Watching her dad and his conduct around Mattie, Jerilyn saw a side of him she had not previously been exposed to. She thought, *like my brothers' unique personalities. No wonder there were always girls around them.*

~

Jon took Linda home after the wedding and learned she would be leaving early the next morning. This time for international flights, and she wasn't sure when she would be home again. Linda had delayed telling Jon, not wanting to detract from the happiness and joy of the wedding.

They were both still in the clothes they had worn for the wedding. Linda asked, "Why don't you go home and change, then come back so we can be together a bit longer?"

When Jon returned, he and Linda took a walk through the neighborhood, quiet as they contemplated the fact they were going to be apart for some time, the longest since they had been together. Then Linda mentioned how everyone at the wedding had reacted to Josh and Jerilyn having their parents as their attendants.

"Yes," Jon agreed. "And they seem to like each other. Too bad they live so far apart."

"So did Josh and Jerilyn," Linda reminded him, then asked, "Have you ever thought your dad might want to be married again?"

Jon hadn't, but he didn't want to talk any more about his dad, instead, wanting to enjoy the small amount of time they had before he had to leave.

~

On Sunday morning, the three from Nebraska were considering what they might do before their mid-afternoon flight. Nancy and her mother were at a hotel while Mitchell spent the few days with his cousin Nate, who lived in Overland Park. All had been invited to church but hadn't indicated whether or not they would attend. Nate would be going to second service as usual and asked Mitch whether he was going or not.

"I'll call Nancy, see what she and her mother want to do."

Nate laughed and said, "After watching Mattie and Jeff Tate at the wedding, she will probably want to go. Though he does usually attend first service."

Jeff was slower than usual getting around and wasn't going to make it to the first service which he usually attended. Remembering his invitation to Martie, he wondered if she would be there. *Did I say anything about there being more than one service?*

What does it matter. She will be leaving in a few hours anyway. But there had been that extra beat of his heart when they danced. Jeff had never expected to feel that again. He had loved Joyce so much and she would always be in his heart.

Perhaps it was opportune that Jeff entered the worship center just as Martie and the young people arrived. Both his and Martie's eyes lit up when they saw each other. He came to her and led her to a seat, leaving the others. Nate's girlfriend, Carly, came in with her parents, so the two couples found seats in another area.

After the service, Jeff and Martie made sure to get each other's contact information so they could keep in touch. And despite anyone who might be watching, they hugged.

Five

In Nebraska, it was late when they arrived home, but there were already plans for Mattie to spend the night with Nancy. She was glad of that because she was tired after the long day and wanted to feel refreshed when she started the drive home to Plattsford. After Mitch delivered them, they had ordered pizza. There had been no meal since breakfast, and they were hungry.

The trip had offered Mattie the opportunity to see the interaction between her daughter and Mitchell Robbins. Before she left on Monday morning, she asked her, "Do you know how your face lights up when you're with your Mitchell?"

Nancy didn't, but she had noticed the same reaction from her mother when she was with Jeff Tate. And there was no question he had been glad to meet her mother.

She had only recently realized how young Mattie had been when her dad died. She didn't know about Jeff. Nancy was sure there had been no man who caught her mother's attention until Jerilyn's dad. Maybe the same was true of him. But could anything come of it? There was a big distance between Overland Park, Kansas, and Plattsford, Nebraska. And somehow, the situation seemed so different than that of her brother, Josh and Jerilyn.

~

The first thing Mattie did when she got home was text Jeff.

"Spent the night with Nancy. Think I told you I was going to. Now I'm home. Not sure what I'm going to do today. Maybe walk around the yard, see what needs to be done with the flower beds. I'm glad I met you, my son's father-in-law. (followed by a heart emoji) *Take care."* She signed it Martie, since that's what he called her.

Josh and Jerilyn were on their honeymoon and wouldn't be in Plattsford until the end of the week. Mattie was grateful she had gotten better acquainted with Jerilyn. But would it be different now, since she had met Jerilyn's dad?

She recalled how surprised she had been when she was introduced to him. That extra warmth as they shook hands, then that grin, remembering her first thought—that it didn't matter what Jeff Tate would be like. Not likely she would ever see him again.

~

Jeff grinned when he got the text from Martie, a good way to begin the day. And he thought, *just like Joyce—she contacted me first.*

Jack and Jon had been at the rehearsal and wedding, and along with their sister, had noted the demeanor between their dad and Josh's mother. Since none were at church the day after, they had missed their continued attention and the hug before Mattie left.

What might they have thought about it? Even Jeff wasn't sure what he thought. He hadn't expected to ever have those warm feelings again. And maybe whatever it was with Martie was because of the circumstances, the wedding of their children. Each had shared their dream of having grandchildren. Now that his daughter and her son were married, maybe that would happen.

He read the text again, wanting to send one to Martie. What would he say? She had said she was glad she met him, and he was certainly glad he had met her. But what could come of it? Though there was that heart emoji …

Before the wedding, before Jerilyn and Josh had made a decision about where they would live, he remembered telling her that Nebraska would be a new place to visit. Maybe seeing Martie would be another reason.

When she sent the text, Martie wondered if Jefferson would send one to her. She even wondered if he texted, *after all he's a man*. But thinking about how she felt about that man, and how that surprised her, she was glad they could keep in touch. But to what purpose with all those miles between them?

Then there was the sound indicating she had received a text.

"I was glad to get your text to start my day—an hour earlier for you. Will have to remember that difference in time. I'm glad I met you too. I haven't taken care of the flower beds here. They need a lot done." He, too, added a heart emoji and signed it *Jefferson*.

Neither Jeff nor Martie considered how short the time was since they had been together. But communication could be immediate these days—different than when they were young, except, of course, for telephone calls. Though even they were easier and more immediate with everyone having their phone in a pocket.

Would they have phone calls? Maybe if they reached a point where they wanted to hear the other's voice. Eventually, Josh and Jerilyn began to write letters in addition to all those other forms of keeping in touch. They liked—even loved—having those pieces of paper with the words written on them, being able to hold in their hands and read over and over.

Jefferson and Martie had barely met, having only minutes—perhaps long minutes—together. Were the emotions which had surprised them strong enough to want to maintain contact, especially writing letters? In one way, that seemed more permanent.

Jeff and Joyce had lived in the same city. Not that many miles separated them—no need or reason for letters. *Still*, he thought, *it would be good to have an old love letter from Joyce to hold and read, to remember again those special times with her.*

Drawing himself back into the present, Jeff thought, *Why am I mooning about writing love letters? If I'm going to write anything, it needs to be a grocery list.*

~

As he started the list, Jeff thought of the recent changes which affected how much he needed. Jack had bought Jerilyn's house and had moved in. There was no question that he and Jayden Black spent as much time together as possible. Might there be a wedding for them soon?

Jon's schedule hadn't changed; his shifts for the Fire Department meant he was away days at a time. Thinking of that, Jeff decided that instead of planning meals for three men, it was more like one and a half.

How long might that last? Jon, too, had a very special lady, Linda Morgan.

With all those thoughts in his mind, it occurred to Jeff that it might not be long before he was living alone.

Somehow, that had not crossed his mind previously. How would it be living alone? Martie had lived alone for years—how many? Does one get used to that? No one to talk to except yourself. No one to help make decisions. Is that good or bad? Seems like it's better to have someone else's opinion, even if you don't agree.

Jeff felt the urge to send another text, or email, or even call Martie, but chose not to when he realized it had only been a few hours since the first one. *Seems like I do want to keep in contact. Maybe I'll make a list for that so I can remember what I want to ask her.*

❧

In Nebraska, Martie read the text from Jefferson again, wondering what he was doing in Overland Park, Kansas. Then as she told him she might, she put on sunscreen, got her straw hat and gloves, and went out to check her flower beds. It was almost September, nearing the end of the growing season, but she wanted them to be in good shape. She carried a trowel with her, prepared to dig out or pull weeds if she found any.

As Martie scrutinized the beds, she wondered what Joyce Tate had grown in her gardens, perhaps some of the same she did. She also remembered wondering if Anita O'Neill might be interested in growing flowers—before she learned Josh would never have any interest in her.

Now I have a daughter-in-law who even got gardening paraphernalia at her shower, ready to learn and honor her mother at the same time.

When she was back in the house, Mattie remembered Jerilyn suggested having a reception in Nebraska when she and Josh were settled, saying, "That would allow us to include your friends who can't come to the wedding."

She had also mentioned it might mean extra work for Mattie, but both she and Nancy agreed it was a wonderful idea. Thinking about that, Mattie figured it would be awhile yet before that could happen. *I'll check with Debra Harris and Emily Warren; see if they might be interested in helping.*

~

Many of the cashiers and others who worked at the store knew Jeff from his shopping trips. He hadn't thought about it before, but it was almost a social gathering when he was there. They even shared family news, so most of them knew about Jerilyn's wedding, making that a topic of conversation with several of them, including the one checking him out. The next person in line seemed interested in hearing about the wedding too. Jeff wondered later if he should have known her.

While he was putting the groceries away, Jeff's thoughts returned to his daughter. She was living on her own before Joyce's death, but he still saw her every Sunday. There were other times, too, when she invited him and her brothers to her house for a meal.

Now he was surprised, feeling a sense of emptiness because she would no longer be in Overland Park. He hadn't expected that. Martie had lost her husband, but both of her kids were in Nebraska. *I've got to remember I told Jerilyn that would be a new place to visit.*

~

Josh and Jerilyn barely got settled in Plattsford before they started school, a few days before the students. Not until then was there a chance to relax from all the wedding preparations, then the honeymoon and the move.

Now came the thought that not only would the students be new to her, so would the parents. Then she remembered Josh's neighbors. She had met some of the kids during her visit in the summer, reminding her that kids are pretty much the same wherever and the same for parents.

That question was settled, then Anita O'Neill came to mind. Would she still be at the school? If she were, how would that be?

Instead of continuing to have apprehension, she took time to pray.

"Father, You know all things and want good for all of us. Now, I thank You for all the blessings You give and ask You to be with me as I begin this new chapter of my life. Help me to accept the many circumstances that will occur and help me face them with love and kindness. In Jesus' name. Amen."

Six

Jeff rarely called his daughter when she lived in Overland Park, but now he found himself wanting to hear her voice, wishing she wasn't so far away. Jerilyn had pledged to keep in touch with her dad but hadn't done so, despite her intention.

She had finished her first week of school, and it was late Friday afternoon when he called.

"Hello, Dad."

"Hello to you. Sure good to hear your voice."

"Yours too."

Jeff wanted to know how school was. Did she like the kids? Did they like her?

She asked him what he was doing to stay busy, thinking he might want to know about Mattie/Martie, but not sure whether to ask. Jerilyn told him, "We're going to have Sunday dinner with Mattie. Nancy will be there too. Not sure about Mitch.

"Think Josh and I will plan to have them all here the week after that."

Jerilyn could almost feel the reaction from Jeff, hearing something about Mattie—Martie to him. Her mother-in-law had asked her if she had heard from him.

Jeff and Martie had both thought about sending another text. After talking to his daughter, Jeff decided it was time, and as soon as the phone call ended, he started to do so but hit the phone icon instead.

He was surprised to hear the ring, but waited, wondering if Martie would answer.

"Jefferson."

"Yes. Just talked to Jerilyn. I'm jealous that you get to see her; no idea I would miss her like I do, but so glad she and Josh got together. And that I met you."

Why did I tell her that? Didn't I tell her before?

"Think I understand your missing her … another kind of separation."

"It is. Well, nothing else to talk about. I guess I wanted to talk to someone who might understand. Glad you answered the phone. Bye."

"Bye."

Why did I hang up so soon, like I was some shy boy, uncomfortable talking to a girl I liked, not knowing what to say?

Mattie was a bit disappointed that the call had been so short and almost brusque, as if Jefferson hadn't intended to call. *Maybe he didn't. Just hit the wrong button. But it was good to hear his voice.*

I could call him. Why don't I? Sending that text was easy, but a phone call is different. What's that word I ran across in that old book? Pusillanimous, meaning timid, cowardly. That's how I feel when I think of calling Jefferson. And why is that? It's not like I expect to have a relationship with him … Do I?

∼

Summer was past. It was the end of September, reaching toward October, when weather was mild but always with the possibility for days to be cooler. Jeff remembered one early October day not that many years ago when they had snow. Still, the former Police Lieutenant, Jefferson Lawrence Tate, needed something to occupy his mind and time.

Well, there was the Overland Park Historical Society, but it was past Fall Festival, so not so many events and activities to keep him busy. It would be spring before most things he participated in started up again, though he did attend most of the monthly meetings. *I need to check when the next one is.*

Maybe I can organize another get-together with the "Old Cops." Jack had been at the last meeting, enjoying reminiscing with them, most of whom remembered when he and Jon were young. That had been several weeks ago, before Jerilyn's wedding. Jack had been enjoying the event until one of the retirees mentioned Jim Murray. He had known him as a new officer about the time of his retirement.

The man said to Jack, "Heard he was your FTO and you were dating his daughter."

It took no time for Jack to confirm Murray was his FTO, but he wasn't dating his daughter. He was very much in love with Jayden Black and wanted to be sure she hadn't heard that rumor. He verified that his phone was in his pocket, then left to be with her. Now they were engaged. Jeff wondered if Jack might want to come to another gathering.

I'll see what his schedule is, maybe plan for a day he is off. Who was it that made that comment? Wonder if he will come?

~

Before he had time to make any further plans about the possibility, Jack was shot. He was on patrol when he was dispatched to an attempted bank robbery. He was the first to arrive, shot before he had time to do any more than draw his gun. Other officers had been dispatched and arrived just as Jack went down. One stayed with him while the others quickly surrounded the would-be robber.

After that first awkward phone call Jefferson made to Martie, there had been others, some he initiated, but at other times, it was Martie. Phone calls seemed to be becoming their main means of communication. Thus, as soon as he let Jerilyn know about her brother, he called Martie.

Just as in all those previous phone calls, Martie felt an increased heartbeat.

"Hello."

"Martie. Wanted to let you know that Jack was shot."

"Oh my. Have you told Jerilyn?"

"Yes," Jeff said. "Don't really know why, but wanted you to know. He was shot in the shoulder and will be in the hospital a couple of days. When he's released, he needs to be where someone can be on hand for any assistance. So he'll be at my house."

"Oh. I'm so sorry he was shot, but glad he'll be okay." When Martie heard that Jack had been shot, she felt disoriented, lost, concerned. How must Jefferson feel, and Jerilyn, and especially Jayden? "Guess you'll get to take care of him."

"Yeah. Haven't had that kind of duty since he was a child. Of course, Joyce did most of that. How are things there? Jerilyn wants to come see her brother. I tried to convince her he'll be okay and maybe she shouldn't miss work," Jeff told her.

"I can understand Jerilyn wanting to see for herself. I think she and Josh, as well as Nancy and Mitchell, will be here Sunday. We may have lunch at Eddie's Café then head back here to visit and share our thoughts and feelings."

"Thanks for your words; I'm glad I can share my concerns with you. I'll call or text later. Bye."

"Maybe I'll call next time. I'll be praying for you and Jack. Bye."

~

Jack would have preferred being at his house with Jayden taking care of him. They all knew and understood, but she had a job; his dad, Jeff, was retired.

Jayden did come every day after work to spend some time with Jack and occasionally picked up lunch for the three of them—at times, the four of them if Jon was off. She and Jack were learning more about each other, he was learning more about his dad, and Jayden was getting better acquainted with her future father-in-law.

They were both surprised how much help Jack needed. He was frustrated, knowing that he was unable to do the simplest things without assistance. Still, he was determined to do everything feasible to heal and regain his independence.

Though he was now a police officer as his dad had been, Jack hadn't questioned Jeff about his law-enforcement career. And his dad hadn't communicated much about it, perhaps as is common for all who share that important occupation.

"So, Dad," Jack began a conversation one of the first days he was in recovery. "I know Grandpa Tate was a police officer. Is that the reason you chose to make that your profession?"

Jeff was reminded of the day his sons asked him about his dating days and when he and their mother met. He had been an officer only a few years when they'd met and had fallen in love immediately.

Back to Jack's current question, he answered, "Probably. My dad was always a hero to me. All police officers were. Plus, there was no other occupation calling me.

"Think I was about ten years old when I decided that was what I wanted to do. My life after that was focused on becoming part of a police department. I remember one day, dad was able to come home for lunch. He took off his shirt and tie, I guess so he wouldn't spill food on them.

"He draped them over a chair where I saw them, decided to try them on, be a policeman. He and mom saw me with his shirt on, tie draped loosely around my neck, and his hat on my head. Mom grabbed a camera to take my picture. It's probably around here somewhere."

"That's what I figured," Jack said. "I know I got sidetracked for a while, thinking I wanted to be a newspaper man. And I enjoyed that. Still, law enforcement was in the back of my mind. I had watched you and your friends and had absorbed the importance of your work.

"I got mad when I saw or heard anyone complaining and thought, *Don't they know how bad things would be without them?* So, even though I never said it, you're my hero."

Both had tears in their eyes as they hugged.

~

Jack was tired and fell asleep. Jeff sat by his side for a bit longer, contemplating the words he had heard, thinking, *You and Jon are my heroes now. Do you know how proud I am of you?*

Seven

On Sunday, Mattie, Josh and Jerilyn, along with Nancy and Mitch, went to Eddie's Café for lunch after church, then to her home for dessert and to spend time together. Much of their conversation was about Jerilyn's brother Jack and his recuperation at his dad's house.

"Jefferson said that since he and Jack are always together, they're having wonderful conversations, remembering past times and talking about the future," Mattie told them.

Nancy and Jerilyn made note of Mattie's reference to Jefferson and turned to each other with questioning looks. Nancy recalled an earlier time when her mother said something about communicating with him.

"So you did call him?"

"Yes. We've talked a few times since the wedding."

Nancy sensed an aura of exhilaration from her mother when she said "Jefferson." And to Jerilyn, her mother-in-law's face reflected an inner happiness she hadn't noticed before. She thought of her father. Might he be feeling the same?

Mattie wondered if her daughter and daughter-in-law were able to sense that extra beat in her heart when she thought about

Jefferson. How had that come to be? It had been years since Andrew's death, and no one since had captured any special attention from her. But that first touch of Jefferson's hand had opened up something in her. She looked forward to each text, each email, and especially the phone calls.

To change the focus of her thoughts, and maybe that of those two, Mattie said, "Jerilyn, we talked earlier about possibly having a reception here for you and Josh. I know you're concerned about your brother, hoping to go see him. But how about the first of November, before Thanksgiving?"

Her daughter-in-law was still absorbing the fact that her dad and Martie—as he called her—were communicating. What might that mean? Her mother-in-law needed an answer, so she told her, "I still want to see Jack. I'll know more after that.

"I know there are things you'll have to check on, like the venue. If I say, 'yes, if' will that create an obstacle if the date has to be changed?"

"No." Mattie said. "We'll include it in the invitation, just in case."

~

Even after Jack's healing, and recuperation, and returning to work, Jerilyn still wanted to see for herself that all was well. She remembered times past when her brothers felt they needed to watch out for her, an accountability they had taken upon themselves. *Guess I'm not so different.*

The school let her miss some in-service days, allowing her time for a trip to Overland Park. With her concern for her brother settled, the reception in Nebraska took place on the date originally suggested.

Looking around at all the guests, Mattie thought, *Wish we could have invited Jefferson; maybe we could have danced again. But would he have come? Maybe I'm dreaming, expecting too much.*

Then she learned that Jack and Jayden were talking about having their wedding soon. His being shot convinced them they didn't want to wait to be together. Though she could think of no good reason why they should, Mattie thought, *Maybe they'll invite me.*

~

A few days later, she sent an email to Jefferson describing the event. He had known about it, and Jerilyn called him afterwards letting him know how she had enjoyed it and telling him about the gifts they had received.

"I've met lots of people since I've moved here; I was introduced to others at the reception."

"That's always a good thing. Hope they're all friendly."

"They are. No question everyone thinks a lot of Josh's family. Nancy and Mitch were there too. I've always loved my brothers, but it's nice to have a sister. Guess when Jack gets married, Jayden will be another. And of course there's Linda too."

"Yeah, our family is growing. And in a short time. So how is Martie? Is she a good mother-in-law?"

"The best," Jerilyn assured him. "She didn't say anything, but I think she wished you were there."

Josh had come to where she was sitting on the couch, sat beside her, reached his arm around her, and pulled her close, put his head against hers, then turned, wanting to give her a kiss.

"Josh wants something, so I'll say bye."

"Tell Josh, Hi."

"I will. Bye."

"Bye."

Josh teased her. "What do you think I want?"

"Dad says, Hi," then she kissed him. "Is that what you wanted?"

"It'll do for now. Everything okay with your family in Kansas?"

"Since Jack will be getting married soon, we talked about how our family is growing."

When she told him that, she noticed his grin and remembered his text when she was in Overland Park checking on her brother. He had told her about Mark and Austen's baby being born, then asked, "When can we have a baby?"

Yes, that was another way families grow.

~

Jerilyn and Josh would be going to his mother's for Thanksgiving. Nancy would join them while Mitchell stayed home to observe the day with his parents and sister, Sandy, and her husband, Ronnie. They were expecting with the baby due in January. His parents, especially his mother, were looking forward to being grandparents. Jerilyn knew that was true also of her father and Josh's mother.

Because Nancy's birthday was close to Thanksgiving, sometimes even the same day, her family had also always celebrated it at the same time, having candles on the pumpkin pie in place of a cake. She learned later that the same was true of Mitchell, except they had a special apple cake for the celebration.

Before she and Josh left to go to Mattie's, Jerilyn called her father. Thinking how the day was different than the year before, she said, "It was still just you and me, Jack and Jon."

"Yes, you cooked, and we three males went to your house. Now you're married, living in Nebraska. Jack is engaged. He's off, so able to spend the day with the Blacks, and Jon is at the Morgans."

"Oh, Dad. I'm sorry you're having to spend the day alone."

"It's okay. They'll be here later with their ladies. Figured they're all having the expected turkey with all the trimmings, so I'm making stew."

"Oh, I remember your stew. It's so good."

~

When she was at Mattie's, Jerilyn learned she had called Jeff earlier. In addition to talking about the meals of the day, he had told her that Jack and Jayden were getting married the week before Christmas. "Did you know that?" she asked Jerilyn.

"Yes. I told him that Josh and I would have a couple of weeks off at that time and could go to his wedding," Jerilyn said, still surprised her father and mother-in-law were communicating—often.

When his sons got to Jeff's, they hugged him instead of shaking hands. Both had just realized how different the day had been from past years and their dad had spent it alone. Jayden and Linda hugged him too. He told them, "I could get used to this."

Before they chose their seats, Jeff asked them to form a circle and hold hands, then he prayed, giving thanks for the day, the meal, and all blessings.

They all loved the stew with dumplings. When they were enjoying dessert—apple cake like Joyce used to make—Linda said, "This is my third Thanksgiving meal. Kate Pearson invited us to an early one when we were in Nebraska. Jerilyn and Josh and his mother were there, too."

"Ah, Martie," Jeff said, then asked, "how is she?"

There were amused smiles on his sons' faces, wondering where the conversation might lead. They had no idea that their dad and Martie were communicating regularly.

Linda told him she was okay and did ask about him. "Mattie said, 'If I'm invited to Jack and Jayden's wedding, I could see him again.'"

None could miss Jeff's smile and the blush on his face when he asked, "Is she?"

Jayden assured him she would be. They had all noticed a certain sadness from Jeff when they arrived, something more than having spent the day alone. After learning that Mattie—Martie—would be invited to the wedding and he would see her again in a few weeks, he wore a happy smile.

~

Their conversations turned to decorating for Christmas. Jack mentioned the Blacks' village they put up each year. They had begun taking the buildings out after their dinner. Jack made a point of checking them out before he and Jayden left.

Jon said, "Since I'm putting up lights on people's houses, maybe we should at least have a tree this year."

Jeff said, "That would be good, been awhile since we did. There's a tree somewhere around. I'll see if I can find it. What about you, Linda?"

"Since there are only adults in the house, we have only had a tree in the living room, not much more than that even when Austen and I were still home, maybe a wreath on the door. I always thought it would be fun to have a village.

"We always went to the Plaza on Thanksgiving night for the lighting ceremony; haven't done that for a few years. Sometime before Christmas, we would drive through several neighborhoods at night to see the Christmas displays and the lights on the houses."

She took Jon's hand, giving him a smile knowing that he would soon be working at adding lights to houses.

"We did that a few times," Jeff said. "Jack and Jon might not remember."

His sons looked at each other and shook their heads. They didn't.

Jayden said, "We didn't go to the Plaza lighting ceremony, but some years, we made a special trip to see them. Several families in Spring Valley have Christmas lights on their houses."

Then she asked Jack, "What are you going to do?"

He took her hand and said, "That depends on you. We'll be together when it's time to undecorate. How about a Nativity this year?"

"I like that," she told him.

"Good. Shall we look for one next week?"

Similar discussions were taking place in Plattsford, Nebraska, with Jerilyn wondering what kind of traditions the Wilsons had. She remembered when her mother was alive, there were a few years when there was more than one Christmas tree, plus an old Nativity that had belonged to her grandmother.

Now she wondered what happened to it. Was it somewhere in her dad's house? He and her brothers had not even put up one tree since her mother died. Jerilyn had one small one she always decorated and had brought it to Nebraska.

She learned that Josh had done no decorating. Nancy's were minimal. But every year, Mattie got a real tree from an organization which sold them as a money-making project. It was decorated with an angel topper that had come from her family. The rest of the ornaments were from several generations, including some that Nancy and Josh had made.

After mentioning them, she glanced at her kids and said, "Maybe someday there will be ornaments made by my grandchildren."

Nancy noticed the distinctive glance between her brother and his wife. Did that indicate some special news? She thought about Mitch's sister who was expecting and how excited Meg and Dennis were about becoming grandparents.

Might I be married next year, hoping for that special event?

Back in Overland Park, Linda had watched Jack and Jayden as they talked about decorating Jack's house. They were not yet together but would be when it was time to put away Christmas.

She wondered if that would ever be so for her and Jon. She loved him and was sure he loved her, but it had not been said. While that was in her thoughts, he leaned down to give her a kiss and with his sweet grin said, "Maybe we'll decorate together some day."

"Will we?"

It had been a long day with family and food, but Jon wanted to spend some time alone with Linda before taking her home, so headed to Starbucks for coffee.

Jon led her to a corner table and when they were settled, said, "There's something I need to tell you."

His demeanor had become so sober, Linda was concerned, not sure she wanted to hear what it was. But she was taken aback when Jon said, "I love you," and he was so happy to learn she loved him too. An unexpected finale to the day with a very special new reason for Thanksgiving.

Eight

*I*n Nebraska, Mattie had received her invitation to Jack and Jayden's wedding, addressed to Martha Wilson. She smiled every time she picked it up to read again, thinking about them and knowing they were so much in love. But mostly, she remembered Jefferson, being with him, dancing with him.

She had picked out a Christmas tree, and it had been delivered and set up for her in the usual corner of the living room. The boxes of ornaments were scattered around, except for the special one that held the angel for the top of the tree. It was in the top drawer of the bureau in her bedroom—the bureau where Andrew's picture sat.

Mattie always put the angel on the tree first, perhaps opposite to what most people did. It was as if the angel had a special spirit to watch over and supervise the rest of the trimming.

She went to the bedroom to get the angel and took it out of the drawer. Holding it in one hand, she picked up the picture of Andrew in the other and carried them both into the living room. She set the box holding the angel on a table, then still holding the picture, sat in a nearby chair.

Oh Andrew. I loved you so much and I still do. But I have met someone I like very much. He's Joshua's father-in-law and lives in Kansas. You were the only one who ever made my heart have an extra beat—until Jefferson. We talk on the phone, and I will see him again before Christmas, at another wedding in Kansas.

It's been so long since I could touch you and feel your arms around me, holding me tight. How I wished I didn't have to let you go those years ago. Now I see your love in your eyes and know that love will always be with me, even when I love another.

Mattie kissed Andrew's picture, then held it against her heart with tears in her eyes, grieving again for that lost love, even as she looked forward with hope to a new one.

~

A few days after Thanksgiving, when Jon was on his two-day shift, Jeff decided there would be no better time to search for the Christmas tree. The season had always been so special to Joyce. When she died, there had been no more decorating. She had been the Christmas angel, bringing the Spirit into the house as she spread reminders of the reason for that special time of year through the house.

That first year without her, he could hardly bear thinking about it, grateful for the church services and the special decorations in the worship center. What did Jack and Jon think, even Jerilyn? She had her own home and always filled it with the trimmings that made it special for the season.

A picture of Joyce rested on the bedside table in his bedroom, the one he had once shared with her. Before beginning the hunt for the tree, Jeff had sat on the bed, taking the photo into his hand, tracing the face of the woman he had loved. He clasped it close to his chest and began sobbing, as if it was a brand-new grief.

~

Oh, Joyce, I loved you so much and that love is still in my heart. I could hardly believe you loved me. Sometimes, since you've been gone, life has been hard to bear as I've longed for your touch and being able to wrap my arms around you. Those feelings will always be with me.

Jerilyn got married in August to a man from Nebraska. That's where she lives now. His mother, Martha—Martie—and I were the attendants. I hadn't met her before, but there was a spark, a special feeling from the time our hands touched, so unexpected. We have kept in touch since the wedding. I'll see her again when she comes for Jack's wedding. I loved you and will always, even if there may be a new love for me.

~

He kissed Joyce's picture, then set it back where it had been, saying, "Love you. Now I need to find the Christmas tree. Jon and I decided we need to put it up this year."

It didn't take much looking to find a tree. Jeff had forgotten there were some years that Joyce put up more than one. He also found a Nativity set he had forgotten about; it had belonged to his mother. Considering for a while, he finally chose one of the tree boxes, then took it and the box with the Nativity to the living room where the tree would be set up.

Before opening the box that held the tree, Jeff studied the one with the Nativity set inside, trying to recall when it had last been part of their Christmas decor. Had Joyce set it up every year and he'd been so indifferent he had made no notice of it?

I'll text Jerilyn; she'll remember. Need to check in with her anyway.

"Hi, have a question I hope you can answer. Jon and I decided to put *a Christmas tree up this year. When I found it, I ran across the Nativity set. It's bothering me that I can't remember the last time we—well, your mother—set it up. Why don't I? Know you will remember.*

Have you got your decorations done? I know you took your little tree with you. Does Josh have anything he's used in the past?

Love you."

Instead of sending a return text, Jerilyn called her dad. She wanted to hear his voice and thought maybe he would like to hear hers.

"Hello, Jerilyn, glad you called."

"Me, too. You asked about the Nativity set. Mom hadn't put it up for a few years. Funny, I've been thinking about it. I remember it belonged to one of my grandmothers, but not sure I ever knew if it was Mom's mom or yours."

"It was mine. I remember always being fascinated by it, trying to connect it with Jesus' birth that we read about in Luke."

"Would I be too selfish if I told you I would like to have it? If I had it here, you and my brothers might not see it again."

"I don't think so," Jeff told her. "I'll check with Jack and Jon, see how they feel. Maybe we could divide it up, but still, only one of you would have the manger."

"Josh and I will be there for the wedding; maybe there will be a time we could talk about it. Except, of course, Jack's time is going to be taken up with a big change in his life."

She wasn't surprised when her dad asked, "Is Martie going to be here?"

"Yes, Dad," she told him.

"Okay. I'm glad you called. Love you."

"Love you, too, Dad. Bye."

"Bye."

~

Jeff got the tree set up but didn't begin decorating. When he found the tree, he forgot about the decorations, so they were still hidden away. He would let Jon go on a hunt for them, then they could decorate it together.

He carried the box with the Nativity set to the dining room table and started emptying it. He unwrapped the donkey, the camels and sheep, thinking back to when he was a child helping his mother set up the scene each Christmas time. Continuing to unwrap each figure—human or animal or angel—he thought of Jerilyn's request to have the set. Perhaps she had helped when Joyce set it up for past Christmases.

He left them and the building spread over the table. Unless there were extra people, as on Thanksgiving, it wasn't used for meals. Besides, he wasn't sure where Joyce had placed it; maybe Jon would remember.

~

In Plattsford, Nebraska, Mattie stood on a stepladder so she could reach the top of the tree, thinking, *Maybe I should have asked Josh to do this for me.* She got the angel placed, then filled the container holding the tree with water. She would give it time to soak up some of the liquid before continuing the decorating. From her conversations with Jefferson, she knew he had an artificial tree. Maybe she would consider that for next year.

Jon had completed his shift and was home. He saw there was a tree set up, but no ornaments and the elements of the Nativity scattered across the table. He went looking for his dad and found him in the kitchen.

"So, Dad, looks like you've started Christmas."

"Yeah. Forgot to check for the ornaments for the tree; thought maybe you would do that?"

"What about the Nativity?" Jon asked.

"I don't remember where your mom set it up, do you?"

"No," Jon said as he continued to eye all the pieces.

Jeff smiled, noticing the obvious question on his son's face, and said, "No, not planning to leave it here. Just reliving some memories. You may not remember that it was my mother's. When I was little, she let me help her.

"Talked to Jerilyn. She said she would like to have it, but that depends on you boys."

Jon said, "If you remember Jack and Jayden are getting their own. Don't know what Linda might think, but I would be glad for Jerilyn to have it."

～

As they had planned, Jack and Jayden went shopping for a nativity set. Before doing so, they had checked through the house to determine where they would set it up and on what surface. Jack had been living there only a short while, and that time was interrupted when he was shot and had to move back to his dad's. The house and furniture had been Jerilyn's before she and Josh got married and she moved to Nebraska.

Unable to find anything they thought might work for displaying the Nativity, Jack and Jayden went shopping. They had already decided it would be good to have an end table for the couch and found one that could serve that purpose when the Nativity was put away after Christmas.

Linda had several flights after Thanksgiving, promising Jon she would be home for Jack's wedding. After their two-day shift, he and Garrett began decorating houses.

Jerilyn had told Linda that she and Josh had started writing letters during their long times apart. Thinking that was a sweet idea, Linda wrote a letter to Jon and mailed it during one of her layovers.

Jon was surprised when he received it but liked the notion, so sent one to her, though the only address he had for her was the one in OP. The letters were special, even though they did continue with texts, emails, and phone calls. As with Josh and Jerilyn, Jon and Linda liked having the letters with them to re-read, maybe trace over the words with their finger.

They had no idea, nor did anyone else, that Jeff had considered how it would be to write a letter to Martie and maybe get one back from her.

Nine

While she finished decorating her tree, Mattie was thinking about the upcoming trip to Overland Park, Kansas, for the wedding of Jack and Jayden. She was glad Josh and Jerilyn were making all the arrangements for the flight and a hotel room for her.

They would be staying with Jerilyn's dad. Jefferson had told them there was plenty of room in his house for her to stay too, somehow not feeling comfortable enough to tell Martie himself. She admitted that she wanted to, but despite their phone calls and texts and emails, she thought, *I haven't been with him enough. I need to know him better, want to know him better, before I would feel comfortable staying there. Maybe after the wedding.*

Part of their planning included taking their Christmas gifts so there would be no need to mail them. The wedding gifts had been ordered and would be delivered. Mattie had learned all in the family enjoyed coffee, so she got some special flavors for each of them. She wanted to get a bit more for Jefferson, but not anything that might reveal her feelings.

Then she thought, *It's Christmas. What better than a Christmas ornament?*

She knew he was having a Christmas tree this year, the first time in a while.

~

Jon had found the ornaments and helped his dad decorate the tree. He couldn't help noticing that though Jeff seemed glad to have a tree again, there were times of tears too. Before Linda, Jon would have been puzzled. Now he understood.

Jeff had Christmas gifts for all of his family, including Josh this year—the usual check, except for Jayden and Linda. Jayden would be his daughter-in-law, and though Linda and Jon weren't engaged, he was sure she would be too, someday. He should get something for them but needed to give some thought to what it should be. He definitely could use some advice, but who to ask? There was Martie, but despite all their communication, he felt that would assume a more personal, intimate relationship.

~

Since Martie would be in Overland Park for the wedding, he wanted to get something for her too, which really created a problem. What would be appropriate? Probably nothing indicating the feelings he had for her and how he was looking forward to seeing her again.

Holding one of the ornaments in his hand before placing it on the tree, Jeff took a closer look at it. He remembered it as one Joyce had special feelings for. *That's it! A Christmas ornament. No matter what might happen, maybe Martie will remember me when she sees it each new Christmas season. I'll go shopping for one tomorrow.*

~

The weeks between Thanksgiving and Christmas are busy any year with decorating, shopping, and perhaps social activities. When a wedding is added, there is more to consider and even less time.

There was much excitement when those people who worked with Jayden and saw her every day learned the date of the wedding. Since it was church, it was also a time of special programs and events, including a blessing tree which held tags listing specific items to purchase for those who might be in need. Jayden would be helping with the wrapping when they were returned.

The Police Department had boxes throughout the city for collecting toys; sometimes an officer attended, taking an opportunity to interact with the public. Jack would be one of those doing so at times when he wasn't on a regular shift.

Thus, in addition to wedding preparations already adding to the busyness of the season, Jack and Jayden had other responsibilities. They were unable to spend as much time together as they would like and beginning to feel lonely for the other.

That led to Jack driving to the church on one of his days off, then heading for Jayden's office; he needed a kiss. He wondered if she could leave, go somewhere for lunch. He surprised her when he walked into her office, walked to where she was in front of her laptop, then pulled her to a standing position to give her a kiss. When they looked up, Pastor Bradley, Shelley, one of the secretaries, and the receptionist were standing at the open door.

"Hi, Jackson," the pastor said. "Good to see you. Hope you two have a good lunch."

~

Time passed as it has a way of doing, and it was finally the night of the rehearsal. Tim, Lucas, and Annie, Jayden's niece and nephews, were chasing each other, sometimes hiding behind Jack. Watching them, Jeff and Martie were each thinking what fun it would be to have grandkids. Jeff took special notice of his kids, one a newlywed, one getting married the next day, and one so very much in love, wondering if there were any plans to have children.

The kids had been told that Jack would be their uncle after the wedding, so at the reception, they danced around saying, "Uncle Jack! Uncle Jack!" When it was time to toss the bouquet, Jayden looked around to see where everyone was, then with her back to the crowd of girls, tossed it. Somehow, it landed on the floor between her sister, Carly, and Linda. Talking to Jon about it later, Linda wondered what that might portend, which Jon called spooky when she explained what portend meant. Also puzzled, Jayden's mother picked it up, thinking to take it home and ask about it later.

When the dancing started, Jeff was glad for the excuse to have Martie in his arms. Anyone paying attention could see how both of them were enjoying the time. As they danced, they talked about seeing each other at weddings, wondering when there might be another one and whether they would be attending.

Martie thought about her daughter, Nancy, and knew she was in love with Mitch and he with her. Perhaps a wedding was in their future. Jeff's mind was on Jon and Linda. They loved each other, but there had been no hint that a marriage might occur anytime soon.

As they considered the many miles between Overland Park, Kansas, and Plattsford, Nebraska, if or when there was a wedding planned by any of the young couples, would they even be invited?

Well, forget about what-ifs, I need to appreciate the now. Knowing

Martie would be leaving the next day, he pulled her closer as those thoughts passed through his mind.

Things changed when Josh and Jerilyn decided to stay in OP the week after the wedding to spend Christmas with Jeff, meaning Martie would be staying too. She was assured there was plenty of room in his house, so left the hotel. Much as she liked the idea of being in Jefferson's home, she still felt somewhat unsettled, as did Jeff, though he was glad to have her there. Martie also was concerned that Nancy would be alone for Christmas in Nebraska.

And she did feel abandoned to an extent, though as soon as Meg, Mitch's mother, learned Nancy was going to be alone, she asked her to "Please come and spend these few days with us."

Nancy was glad to do so since she had helped them with their Christmas decorations. To spend that extra time with Mitch was a special gift. Though it seemed he was more excited that he was going to be an uncle in January when his sister's baby was born. Nancy thought, *I would be excited to be a wife*, though there was not yet an engagement.

~

To keep things in a somewhat normal context, Jeff, Josh, Jerilyn, and Martie went to church together on Sunday. Jon would be on duty Monday with Linda leaving on a flight that would take most of the week. He picked her up for church and, on the way, told her about the change of plans. They all got to church at the same time and decided to sit together with Jeff being sure to have Martie sitting beside him.

After church, they all went to Cinzetti's for lunch. Jeff was thinking, *I probably need to get some groceries this afternoon*. He hadn't expected to have house guests for a week more.

When they got back to his house, he started checking through the refrigerator, freezer, and cabinets to see what there was and determine what was needed.

Jerilyn walked into the kitchen while Jeff was making his search and asked, "What's going on, Dad?"

"Making a list for groceries. Haven't done much cooking lately, and out of just about everything for making meals."

"Oh, sorry. We didn't think of that. Why don't you let Josh and me go shopping? We can take your list; we might add some things."

"Oh, well. I guess so. What about Martie?"

"She can stay here," Jerilyn told him. "Finish unpacking, spend time with you getting better acquainted." The last said with a secretive grin.

Jeff wasn't sure how he felt about being in his house alone with Martie. *How long will it take her to unpack? Probably not long since she had expected to be in OP only a few days, thus only a few things to unpack.*

By the time Jerilyn and Josh left, Martie had already finished her unpacking. She was glad to be in Jefferson's home, though it was like a dream. They had danced, but somehow, this seemed to be a closer connection, just the two of them for an hour or so.

Can't hide in here any longer. Father, be with me as I walk through Jefferson's house to find the man I think I'm falling in love with. Surprised at her thoughtful prayer, Mattie admitted to herself, *Yes, I am,* so was smiling as she entered the kitchen where he was still sitting, nursing a cup of coffee as he stared out the window.

Mattie stood quietly, her eyes resting on Jefferson, feeling an increased heartbeat at the confession she had made to herself. How could that be, and what could come of it? They still lived a long distance apart, as had Josh and Jerilyn, but they were much younger. Did that make it easier to make big changes in their lives?

Not wanting to startle Jefferson but wanting to be close to him, Martie knocked on the open door. He turned with a happy smile when he saw her.

"Martie. Did you finish unpacking?"

"Yes, and thinking I need to go shopping, not near enough clothes for a week."

"I bet Jerilyn has the same problem. Maybe you can go together."

He gestured for her to join him at the table. "Would you like some coffee?"

"I would."

"Cream, sugar?"

"No, black is fine."

"Sorry, nothing to go with it. Maybe the kids will bring something from the store. I know you weren't expecting to be away from home for Christmas. Will that create any problems?"

"Not really," Martie said. "Neighbors will keep an eye on my house. Nancy was more surprised than upset. She won't have to celebrate by herself; she'll be at the Rocking R, that's the Robbins' ranch. And she will like that; I only learned recently how despondent she was when we had to leave the ranch. Of course, she will be with Mitch."

Jeff asked, "What about his parents?"

"Think they love Nancy, and she sure likes them."

Ten

Jon spent more time at the station, even worked one man's shift who had just become a new father. Though he did enjoy watching his dad watch Martie when he was home. Linda was on a flight that would take most of the week, but she expected to be home for Christmas. He was glad to have something to occupy his time and mind as he waited again for her to be home.

But, close as it was to the day, he was bemoaning the fact he didn't yet have a gift for her and asked his sister, "Jerilyn, can you help me? I have no idea what to get for Linda."

"How about a bracelet?" she asked. "I think most of us females like them, especially if they're from someone we love."

Jon found one with a silver chain and interlocking hearts, reminding him of his love for her, and hoped Linda would feel it.

~

Donna Morgan had seen all of them, Jerilyn, Josh, and his mother at church and visited with them briefly. Afterwards, Linda told her about the change of plans; they were staying with Jeff Tate through Christmas.

After Linda left for her scheduled flight, Donna thought about what her daughter had told her. Richard noticed the contemplative look on her face and asked, "What's on your mind?"

"Huh?"

"You look like you have a big problem to solve."

"Josh and Jerilyn and Mattie are staying until Christmas."

"So?"

"I know that hadn't been planned. Jeff may not have even thought yet about a Christmas dinner."

"Again, why is that concerning you so much?"

"It looks like Linda and Jon may be a permanent couple, married someday," Donna told him. "That would make us sort of an extended family. How about inviting all of them here for that day, at least for a meal?"

Richard went to his wife to give her a hug. "Sweetheart, as always, you are thinking of others—one of the many things I love about you.

"That's a wonderful idea. And I'll help you as much as I can."

"I know you will," Donna said. "I'll send a text to Jeff tomorrow."

Jeff was glad to receive the text from Donna Morgan. She was right, he hadn't considered having a special Christmas dinner the end of the week. Mostly, he was thinking about each day, one at a time, and what was needed for that day.

He thought, *It will also give us an opportunity to get better acquainted, learn more about each other. That will be a good thing, since Jon and Linda may be married someday.* The same thought that Linda's mother had.

～

None of those in the Tate's house arose early on Christmas morning, probably usual when all were adults. Further ambience of the season, a fireplace with a burning fire and carols playing, was provided by one of the television stations. A good background for the beginning of the day.

Since they would be going to the Morgans' for a meal later in the day, they had brunch, which included many of their favorites. Orange juice, biscuits and gravy, bacon, a quiche, scrambled eggs, and the requisite coffee. There were cinnamon rolls later to go with a second cup.

Both families had their gift exchange that afternoon. Earlier, Jeff had pondered what his usual gifts for his family were, thinking maybe it was time to consider something different. Now, when they opened the cards with the usual Christmas check inside, then thanked him, he felt discomfited. His family was growing, maybe he should start giving "real" gifts, perhaps some small thing even if he continued with the checks.

He had considered getting some small gift for Linda since she might be a daughter-in-law someday; but no idea what it could be, or what would be appropriate. Then he ran across a devotional book that Joyce had loved and thought that would be perfect. When he got the one for Linda, he also got books for Jayden and Jerilyn, knowing how important the verses and words had always been for his wife.

He left the gift for Martie under the tree, still unsure about giving it to her. How would she react? Should it have been something more? He received a book from Jon, *Undaunted Courage* by Stephen E. Ambrose, about the Lewis and Clark expedition. Jack and Jayden gave him a gift card for Cinzetti's before their wedding. Jerilyn and Josh had ordered a new reclining chair for her dad; they were sorry it hadn't been delivered yet. They showed him a picture. He liked it and told them, "I'll probably spend too much time in it."

All were anxious to try the coffee Mattie had given them. Jon received one called Cookie Dough that included cinnamon and hazelnut. There were gifts in Nebraska for Josh and Jerilyn, but they got a sample too—Hazelnut Praline. She had brought a pecan flavor for Jack and Jayden, and for Jeff, there was Maple Bacon. She hadn't tried any of them so couldn't give a report on their taste, though she did wonder.

Josh, Jerilyn, and Martie had not brought their gifts to each other, expecting they would be celebrating at home. They hadn't planned to still be in Overland Park.

"We'll get to have Christmas again; maybe Nancy and Mitchell will join us," Jerilyn said.

There was still the other gift for Jeff. Since being in his house, Martie had checked out the ornaments on the tree and thought it would look good with the others. But just as Jeff was uncertain about giving her the gift he had for her, so was she hesitant. They weren't sitting near each other, but there had been surreptitious glances between them since the gift exchange had begun.

Jon stood and said, "I want to go ahead to the Morgans' so I can take Linda's gift and spend some time with her before we eat." He retrieved the gift from beneath the tree, gave it to his dad, and said, "Looks like you two still have some gifts to exchange. I'm curious. It's none of my business, but I'd like to see what they are."

Martie and Jefferson were unsure why they felt as they did. The gifts certainly couldn't be considered personal, but each knew there were unique special feelings when they chose them. Still, they hadn't expected to be together when they were opened. Did being together on Christmas Day add a different element to everything?

Josh, who was sitting beside his mother, stood and said, "Jeff, I'll trade places with you. Come on over."

Jeff didn't move even when his son-in-law reached him. There had been those glances between him and Martie during the exchange of gifts. But he was still hesitant, not knowing the reason.

Finally, Jerilyn said, "Dad, I know you spent time thinking of something special you could give to Mattie, and I know she did the same."

It was obvious he still felt uncomfortable, but got up and walked over to Martie, then sat beside her. It was the closest they had been to each other since she arrived, though she had been living in his house for a week and was with him in his car when they drove around to see Christmas decorations in the metro area.

At none of those times were they as close as when they had danced. And they had quickly gotten past those first awkward feelings of the day she moved to his house from the hotel. Why was this simple thing creating undefined feelings? Was it because they hadn't chosen a gift for a special person since they had lost the spouse they had loved so much?

They turned to each other and smiled, wondering why they had been so reluctant. Jeff handed his gift to Martie and took the one from her. There was another glance, then they unwrapped the gifts at the same time.

Jeff's gift was a gold sleighbell ornament for his Christmas tree. The one for Martie was also an ornament—a metallic snowflake with rhinestone glitter. They held them up at the same time, saying "It's perfect!" then reached toward each other for a hug and a "Merry Christmas!" Finally once again beginning to feel relaxed with each other.

~

Linda had been on a flight, and it had been almost a week since she and Jon had been together. She was glad he came earlier so they could be alone and exchange their gifts before the rest of his family arrived.

There was the bracelet for Linda as Jerilyn had suggested; and just as Jerilyn had predicted, she loved it. Holding it up, she asked, "Will you fasten it for me?"

For Jon, there was a book about dinosaurs—more for a child—but when she bought it, Linda was remembering their visit to Prairie Fire Museum and his interest in them. There was also a picture of her when she was about ten years old.

"I don't have any recent ones," she told him.

It was in a silver frame with silver hearts randomly attached. He loved it and thought, *If we have a little girl, this is what she will look like.*

~

Josh, Jerilyn, and Martie all drove to the Morgans with Jeff in his SUV. Jerilyn had brought a box of special Christmas candies for them and gave to Donna when they arrived. There was also the wrapped devotional book for Linda.

Donna and Richard had first met Josh's mother at his and Jerilyn's wedding and spent time with her when they visited their daughter in Nebraska before Thanksgiving. Now Donna said, "I've heard people calling you Mattie and, sometimes, Martie. What would you prefer?"

She was told, "My name is Martha, and everyone started calling me Mattie when I was little. Then I met Jefferson—Jeff—when I came for Josh's and Jerilyn's wedding. He told me I didn't look old enough to be Mattie, thought I looked more like Martie." She glanced toward him when she said, "And I like it."

"Then we'll call you Martie, too. Now, let's eat."

When they were all seated at the table, Donna asked Richard to say grace.

"Father, we thank You for this time of year and this special day when we celebrate the gift of Your Son. May we remember to be grateful for all the blessings we receive from You. Be with us and all those we love. Now, we thank You for this food; bless it to the nourishment of our bodies. Amen."

~

There was much conversation along with the meal. Donna said, "I haven't heard anything about whether Jack and Jayden planned a honeymoon; did they?"

"They didn't plan to have one, at least anything that required leaving town," Jerilyn told them. "But after seeing commercials on TV, they decided to go to Branson. They will probably be home tomorrow."

"Ah … haven't been there for some time, but those commercials sure make one think," Donna said. Turning to her husband, she said, "Maybe we should plan a trip for next year."

Josh said, "Living in Nebraska, we never actually even heard of Branson. Does seem like people could have fun with all they offer." Then he asked Jerilyn, "Have you been there?"

"We had a family vacation there when us kids were still pretty young," she told him. "They have added a lot since then."

~

When they were having dessert, Donna asked Martie, "Have you done anything interesting, exciting this week?"

"We did. Drove to the Plaza to see the lights. Jon took us around to see some of the houses he had decorated. Watched the birds; saw some I don't remember having seen. And I had to go shopping. Didn't bring enough clothes for a week."

Reacting to Martie mentioning seeing the houses, Jon said, "Yeah, another week and I get to start taking them down. Probably won't be nearly so much fun."

Richard asked, "When are you all heading back home?"

His question caught the attention of Jeff. Though there had been a few uncomfortable times, he had still been glad to have Martie in his home, something he would never have expected.

Josh said, "Tomorrow afternoon. Glad we flew, wouldn't look forward to starting a drive that far this time of year when there could be snow."

"Do you think there will ever be a time when you drive?" Donna asked.

"Maybe in the summer," he answered. "Since we're both teachers, we would have more time. Not like Mark and Austen. As you know, that's when they're the busiest. But, if things continue as they have been, I will probably be spending time at TrailWays too."

"I would like to see the country between here and Plattsford," his mother said. "Until now, there's never been a reason to take a long car trip. Austen was sure brave to do that with just her and David." Reaching for her daughter-in-law's hand, she continued, "Then Jerilyn and her friend drove that long way and hardly had time to rest before heading back to Overland Park."

Martie's words were puzzling to some of those who heard them. What reason might she be pondering? Josh and Jerilyn were living in the same town as she. Perhaps unconsciously a visit to see Jefferson Tate was on her mind. He certainly had in mind to visit Plattsford, Nebraska. His daughter being there gave a good reason and an excuse to make such a trip, knowing he would see her mother-in-law too.

Jeff and Martie, as well as Josh and Jerilyn, went to first service at church on Sunday, then to Dragon Inn for lunch. There was just enough time when they returned to Jeff's house to finish packing and call an Uber for their trip to the airport.

Jerilyn and Josh hugged her dad, then walked toward the door, hesitating before exiting. It was then that Martie and Jefferson moved toward each other and hugged, both with tears in their eyes.

Their arms were still around each other when Jeff told her, "I'm glad you decided to stay with me."

Martie agreed. "Me, too."

"Keep in touch," Jeff asked.

"I will."

Then the hug deepened, as if they were loath to part, and they looked into each other's eyes as if they wanted it to be more but finally separated. They walked to the door together, joining their children, who were outside with all the luggage just as the Uber arrived.

Jeff stayed at the door, watching as the three got settled in the car, then as they headed down the street being carried away. When might he see them again? He could think of no reason that it would be soon. Winter had just begun and it could be a cruel season.

The three in the Uber were silent, Jerilyn and Josh holding hands as they watched his mother. There was no question that she had been sad to leave, reminding them of how they had felt each time they separated, especially after Mark and Austen's wedding. There had been no kiss even though they'd both wanted one.

Was Martie's feeling for Jeff as strong as theirs had been for each other, or was it just a reaction to the circumstances?

Eleven

eff watched until the Uber carrying them was out of sight, lonely already when he stepped back into his house, empty now. He had become accustomed to being alone much of the time—thought he was used to it. Now he questioned that belief. Yes, there are advantages to not having to think of anyone else but somehow a feeling of contentment when others are sharing your space.

When Josh and Jerilyn decided to stay the week until Christmas and Martie joined them, there was a different mood, not worrying, but not usual either. He might as well admit to himself it was not easy to hold back from kissing Martie after their hug. What would she have thought? It did seem like she might have wanted one.

~

Martie was glad her son and daughter-in-law didn't have any questions. She had really wanted Jefferson to kiss her, and she would have kissed him back. Would that ever happen? Was she foolish to even think about any possibility of them being together, even seeing each other, let alone dream about it?

Whatever, she could still text, email, call occasionally when she wanted to hear his voice. She had overheard Jerilyn and Linda talking about writing letters at times when they weren't with their love. Maybe she would mail one to Jefferson. What might he think of that? She and Andrew had not written letters. No need as they could pretty much see each other whenever, and they did often.

Might Jefferson send one in reply? *I would like to have one that I could read anytime I wanted. I could print the emails, but that wouldn't be the same.*

⁓

Martie still had a melancholy feeling when they landed in Scottsbluff—so much so that Jerilyn noticed and was concerned. She wondered, *Might Dad be sad also? I need to call him when I get home, not just send a text or email.*

Her memories returned to the time she had flown back to Nebraska for Austen's wedding. Josh picked her up, she spent the few days with him, then how she felt about him when she left to return to Kansas. Jerilyn wished there had been a kiss. Did Mattie—Martie—feel that way? Did her dad?

They had driven Mattie's car to the airport, leaving their pickup at her house. When they got there, they removed all the luggage and the Christmas gifts they received in Overland Park. Josh carried his and Jerilyn's to the pickup, then picked up his mother's things and walked her to her door.

"Would you like for me to come in with you, make sure all is well?"

Mattie surprised him when she said, "Yes, I would."

She had been an independent, take care of myself woman for

many years. What had caused the change? Jerilyn was standing at the pickup when Josh waved, indicating he would be back out soon, then, still holding the luggage, followed his mother into her house. It was colder and windier than it had been in Kansas, so she climbed in, thankful that Josh had unlocked it before helping his mother.

~

Jeff looked at his Christmas tree, glad Jon had talked him into having one. With the company, it had added an extra festive mood, but now he was feeling sad. How was it that such few changes in one's routine could affect how they dealt with the days?

He thought, *I'll call someone* but could think of no one available. He had lost track of Jon's schedule but knew the soonest he would be home would be the next morning. He wouldn't call him unless it was an emergency. Jerilyn was flying home. Jack was still on his honeymoon. The only other person he would want to talk to, maybe the only one he would really like to talk to, was Martie, who was also on her way home.

Why did I feel so nervous when we exchanged gifts? She had been here all week, but yesterday seemed different, kind of like it was a beginning, even though she was going to be gone.

~

Josh and Mattie stepped inside her house. She closed the door as he looked around.

"Looks like everything's okay in here. Where do you want me to put this?" raising his arms holding the luggage.

"Just set them there," pointing to an area, "then walk through the house with me."

Before they started the tour of the house, he asked her, "Would you like for me to plug in the lights on the tree?"

"No. It's been more than a week since water was added to the container. It's probably dry; don't need a fire."

Josh and his mother walked through all the rooms where everything was in good order, but Josh noticed there were tears in Mattie's eyes.

"Are you okay, Mom?"

"Why?"

"You're crying."

"I'm sorry, just thinking how good it was to be in a house interacting with all of you. It hadn't bothered me before, living alone, have for a long time. It's like I'll have to get used to it again."

"Do you want to come home with us?"

Mattie smiled through her tears, then hugged her son. "Oh, Josh, I'll be okay. Now you need to get on home. Jerilyn may be getting cold sitting out in your truck. Love you both so much."

They had walked to the door as Mattie was talking, then she watched until Josh got to the pickup. She waved as they backed out of the driveway, then headed toward their home.

Maybe I'll call Jefferson. But hearing his voice might make me even sadder. Besides, it's an hour later there and he may be asleep.

~

Jerilyn called her dad while she waited for Josh.

"Jerilyn, so glad you called. I needed someone to talk to."

His daughter sensed some sadness. "I wanted to see how you are after having a houseful of us for a week."

"I'm glad," he replied. "So where are you?"

"I'm in our pickup, waiting for Josh. We're at Mattie's."

"Martie, how is she?"

"Okay, think she wanted Josh to be with her when she went in, probably check to see all is okay."

"Was it?"

"Don't know. He hasn't come back out yet. How are you? It seemed to me you might have been sad when we left."

"Yes," Jeff admitted. "Got kind of used to having you all here."

"What about Mattie—Martie?"

"Yeah."

It was obvious to Jerilyn that he didn't want to say more. "Josh is coming out now. Take care, glad we got to be with you. Love you."

"Me, too. Bye."

∼

Jeff deliberated for a while, then knowing Martie was home, waited no longer to call. She was looking at her tree and thinking about the ornament Jefferson had given her when the call came. Surprised, but glad, she answered.

"Jefferson."

"Yes. Jerilyn called, so I knew you were home."

"Just barely—glad to be home as always—but did enjoy being with you." There was a short pause before she continued, "All of you—a full house."

"I liked having you here, too," Jeff told her. "Everything okay? Jerilyn said Josh had gone in with you to check."

Martie assured him, "Yes. Probably won't have the lights on anymore on the tree; it's kind of dry, don't want a fire. Guess that's an advantage to having an artificial one."

"Yeah," Jeff agreed. "But the fresh ones have such a nice fragrance. Well, won't keep you any longer, glad we got to talk."

Martie said, "Me, too. Take care."

"I will—bye."

"Bye."

Both of them still feeling sad after the call but happy, too, that they had been able to talk to the other at the end of the day.

~

Jeff was in the kitchen, wondering what to have for breakfast. *What did I have yesterday and the day before that?* There was always coffee, and as he was remembering the previous few days, had filled the pot with water and scooped coffee into the basket. It was the Maple Bacon that Martie had given to him. He liked the smell, what might it taste like?

When it finished brewing, he poured a cup and carried it into the living room. Looking at the tree, he contemplated how much longer he should leave it up. It had been a month, or close to it, since they set it up and decorated it right after Thanksgiving. He had added the ornament from Martie, and reached to remove it.

With the ornament in one hand and coffee in the other, he returned to the kitchen, and pulled a chair out from the table. When he sat, he took a sip of the coffee, cooled enough to drink now but still almost hot as he preferred it.

Ah, a different taste. I like it. I should have something more, not just coffee.

Instead, he picked up the ornament for a closer look, remembering how he felt when he and Martie exchanged gifts, so different from the way he acted. It would have been so different if it were only the two of them. *Will it ever be?*

~

Martie had got a sample of the Maple Bacon coffee for herself when she got the others. She hadn't tried it yet, and thinking, *no better time than now*, she got it started, a slice of bread went into the toaster, butter and orange marmalade ready to spread on it.

The only thing she had unpacked was the ornament Jefferson gave her. Martie first thought to put it on the tree, but it had stayed in the pocket of her robe. When it finished brewing, she took her coffee and toast to the table, then removed the gift from her pocket and placed it beside them.

Bowing her head, she said, "Thank You, God, for this food and the safe trip returning us home. May we be grateful for all your blessings as You watch over us. In Jesus' name, amen."

Martie took a sip of her coffee, thinking, *Ah, tastes as good as it smells. Wonder if Jefferson tried his yet. I'll text him later to find out.*

With that man on her mind, Martie picked up the ornament he had given to her, removing it from its box to hang it on the tree. The lights wouldn't be plugged in, but she could imagine how it would sparkle and reflect their light.

Since she, Josh, and Jerilyn had been in Kansas for Christmas, there were still gifts under the tree, waiting to be distributed. Thoughts were marching through Martie's mind. *When shall we have the rest of our Christmas and where? Nancy and Mitchell need to be included too.*

Twelve

Jerilyn had been awake for a while; glad to be home and in her own bed. Josh was still asleep on his side with his back to her. She marveled that she was living in Nebraska with a man she loved so much, something she would never have dreamed of. There was a man in college she had cared for and was sure she loved him. She could hardly bear it when he graduated, moved back east and she never heard from him again. Perhaps that was the reason there had been no one else until Josh.

There was no reason to get up. They had another week off before school started. A decision still needed to be made as to when they and Mattie would have their Christmas with Nancy. Jerilyn expected her mother-in-law would be working on that.

Now she cuddled closer to Josh, remembering that time in the summer when they had fallen asleep on the couch. He stirred, moving slightly, turned over, wrapped her in his arms, then fell back into a deep sleep. In a few moments, so did she.

~

Wanting to settle plans for the rest of their Christmas, Martie decided to start the process by texting Nancy and Jerilyn with her thoughts. Nancy was probably at work, but she would contact her first, thinking, *Mitchell needs to be included too. Being on the ranch, with its needs, his time is probably the most limited. Maybe we could meet at Nancy's; he wouldn't have to drive so far. I'll ask her, see what she says before contacting Josh and Jerilyn. I need to let her know we're all safely home anyway.*

"I'm home. We need to decide when to have our Christmas. I have ideas, too much for a text. Call when you have time to talk. Love."

Nancy was glad to hear from her mom and sent a return text saying only, *"Good, will call when I'm home."*

She had been away from her home for several days, having spent Christmas with Mitch and his family. It was almost dark when Nancy got home the day before. In fact, she hadn't unpacked her suitcase yet but made sure to have the silver bell Mitch had given to her "for you to ring when you need me."

Would it really work? *I will always need you*, ringing it as she finished the thought. And it must have worked. Her phone beeped; it was a text from Mitch. *"Miss you, wondering how your day was. Call me when you can. :heart emoji:"*

Knowing a call to her mother would probably take some time, she chose to call Mitch first.

"Hello, love."

How Nancy loved hearing that from him. "Hello. Day was okay, not very busy. That was probably good; my mind was on you."

"And mine was on you."

Nancy said, "I need to call Mom. She wants to make plans for the rest of our Christmas. That will include you."

"Hadn't thought of that," Mitch said. "When will it be?"

"Don't know. What would be best for you?"

"Not sure. You know how it is on a ranch."

Nancy said, "I do." Replaying those words in her mind, she wondered, *will there be a time I will say them at a wedding?*

There was silence from Mitch. He was remembering the day Nancy told him, "I love you," and how it affected him.

Then he asked, "How about you and your mom discuss possibilities and get back with me?"

"Okay. She may be wondering why I haven't called yet. So, talk to you later?"

"Absolutely. Love you."

"And I love you. Bye."

"Bye."

~

While deciding what to have—or whether to have—breakfast, Jeff realized there were things he needed. A list was probably not necessary. It was back to just him and Jon, and what he got at the grocery store was pretty much the same every week. Still, so he wouldn't forget anything, he took his pen and a note pad and started writing things down.

While doing so, he thought about Martie. What different things might be included if she was with him? Did she have a favorite cereal? Did she even eat cereal? Again, his mind returned to his earlier thoughts. He couldn't remember what he had for breakfast those days she was here. Though he was so very conscious of her presence, there was no remembrance of what she ate.

He finally made toast to have with his warmed-up coffee, again with the sleighbell ornament on the table in front of him. Taking a bite of the toast, he looked toward the tree, thinking, *It's been there long enough. I'll get the box for the ornaments and start the undecorating. I'll let Jon take care of the tree.*

∾

When Nancy called her mother, they talked first about how Christmas for them had been—different—in separate places. Might that become the normal—with Josh being married, Nancy hoping to be, and what about Martie? There was no question she had special feelings for Jefferson Tate.

Her mother said, "Thinking about when and where we might have the rest of our Christmas, how about your house? It wouldn't be so far for Mitchell to come."

Nancy hadn't expected that and remained quiet.

"Nancy?"

"I guess that would be okay. When?"

"How about the last day of the year, New Year's Eve? Will you have to work that day? Or we could plan for the first day of the new year—a good beginning? Of course, it still depends on Mitchell's schedule as well as yours."

Still no response from Nancy.

"Well, think about it. I don't want to distress you. If it's easier, I would be glad to have all of you come to me. Good to talk to you. Love you."

"Love you, too, Mom. Bye."

"Bye."

∾

After the call, Mattie glanced at her Christmas tree and thought, *I need to get the ornaments off, then see if Josh can come take it down and take it to that place in town where people drop off their trees.*

~

Jeff got to the store with his list, but walked up and down the aisles, checking everything, still wondering what different things he might purchase if Martie was with him—and why was that? He was a man in his fifties, not some young man—or boy—with a new crush, dreaming about being together.

But I do have that crush. What can I do about it? What might Martie think of it—seems like she might feel the same. How might she react if I told her—I do want to hear her voice. Maybe I'll call when I get home. Now I need to get these groceries.

A woman shopper had noticed Jeff and watched the changing expressions pass across his face. "Hello, Jeff," she said to him. "Looks like you have some serious thoughts on your mind."

Surprised, Jeff gave his attention to the woman. She was the same one who had made the comments about Jerilyn's wedding those few months ago. He still thought she looked familiar, but no idea why.

She continued, "Maybe it's because there was recently another wedding."

"Maybe."

"You haven't attended the OPHS meetings for a few months. Maybe you can make the one in January?"

Ah. That's why he recognized her, but still didn't remember her name. Jeff did no more than nod his head, and the woman, realizing that's all she would get, said, "Good seeing you again," and headed toward the front to check out.

~

It was decided the extended Christmas for the Wilsons would be held at Nancy's on the last day of the year—New Year's Eve. Instead of anyone needing to cook, they would order meals from Runza's to be delivered.

She told Mitchell it was the first time she would host a get-together at her home when she called to give him the details. He asked, "How did that come to be?"

"As far as family, there was just Mom, Josh, and me. It seemed to be automatic to go to Mom's, even though both Josh and I had our own place.

"Thinking about it, I don't have enough dishes and silverware for that many people. Maybe I'll get some of those fancy disposable ones."

~

Martie had continued to be on Jeff's mind while he placed items in the cart at the grocery store. They hadn't been in touch since that night she got home after the week spent at his house. *That's only a few days, seems longer.*

Before he had a chance to get in touch with her, Jeff received an email from Martie. "It's been less than a week since we had Christmas at your house, but you've been on my mind. We've decided to have the rest of the Wilson Christmas at Nancy's on New Year's Eve. Guess I should say Wilson and Robbins; Mitchell will be with us too. I wonder what next Christmas will be like. Probably not as spread out as this one has been. My tree is still standing. I took the ornaments off, waiting for Josh to take it down.

"I got some of the Maple Bacon coffee for myself. I like it, have you tried yours yet? What will you be doing the next few weeks? I don't have anything planned; sometimes winter weather and snow interfere with plans anyway."

~

After reading the email from Martie, Jeff called her instead of sending a return one. He wanted to hear her voice anyway.

"Jefferson!" Martie sounded happy that he called.

"Yes. Got your email, had been thinking about sending one to you, but decided I had too much I wanted to say. Too much for an email. Sounds like you're still having Christmas."

Martie answered, "Yes, though there aren't really many gifts to exchange. Think I just wanted to have some time with my kids before they all get back into their usual routines."

"I understand that," Jeff told her. "Lots of changes already, maybe more before next Christmas. You asked about the coffee, I had some for breakfast. I like it. Thanks again.

"You wondered what I would be doing the next few weeks. As you said, it's winter, and that changes things. I haven't done much with the Overland Park Historical Society for some time. Not much happening except meetings until spring, but they usually have great speakers, and there would be other old-timers to visit with."

"Old-timers," Martie said. "Do you consider yourself one of them?"

Jefferson said nothing for a while, then, "Guess I have for some time. But not when I'm with you."

After those unexpected words, neither knew what to say, then from him, "Guess that's enough for now, good to talk to you."

"You too, take care."

No goodbyes from either of them, but Jefferson in Overland Park and Martie in Plattsford continued to hold their phones— those words from Jeff in their minds. They washed over Martie. She felt the same when she was with him. Was it foolish to have those feelings?

Their children were married to each other, but that didn't mean Martie and Jefferson would ever be a couple. Then she laughed and thought, *weddings have brought us together, but how many more will there be, and will we both be attending?*

Jeff wondered, *why did I say that?* Yes, they truly expressed his feelings, but he hadn't meant to blurt them out. *Martie said nothing—so she must not feel the same.*

~

Martie sat with the phone still in her hand for a few more minutes, then stood, thinking, *I need to check, see if I need any groceries, pull myself back into real life—stop dreaming like a teenager.*

Thirteen

Winter crept into Nebraska and Kansas, and despite the special feelings Jefferson and Martie had for each other, communication had stopped. He felt he had shared too much of himself in the statement he made during that phone call.

And, though Martie felt the same as him, there was some confusion for her too. Did Jefferson not want to have those feelings? Realizing how long it had been since they were in touch, she decided it was time to do something. Maybe something different would elicit his attention.

A few days later, Jefferson was surprised to receive a letter from her. He was hesitant about opening it. What might it mean? Though his thoughts did return to that time a few months ago when he considered what it would be like to have a letter from someone he cared for.

He had just returned from the monthly meeting of the Overland Park Historical Society. The woman who had made a point of greeting him when he was getting groceries was also in attendance and had taken a seat next to him.

"Jeff. So good to see you here. All of us have missed seeing you. So no more weddings?"

"Not for a while," he answered, still unable to recall the woman's name. Despite her efforts, he wasn't interested in carrying on a conversation. Thinking of Martie, wondering why he had stopped calling, or texting, or at least sending an email. He hadn't heard from her either. *I'm going to change that. I'll call her when I get home.*

But when he got home, there was the letter. He studied her handwriting on the envelope—beautiful, not like the almost block printing of so many these days, including him and his kids, not that any of them wrote very much. Though he had overheard Linda and Jon talking about their letters to each other when they were parted for long periods of time.

Jeff held the letter in his hand, still reluctant to open it, afraid of what the words might be. Finally, he carefully opened the envelope and pulled the letter out.

Dear Jefferson,

I have missed our communicating. Not sure what happened— maybe those words of yours—'when I'm with you'—made us both wonder.

Whatever, I know it's not something either of us expected. Should we just look forward to other weddings? Who knows when that might happen? Have there been any proposals? You do have a daughter here.

Maybe you can come for a visit?

Guess that's enough for you to think about for now. I look forward to hearing from you.

Love,
Martie

When she wrote the letter, Martie thought, *This is the first time*

I've written to a 'boy' I like. In Kansas, Jeff smiled, thinking, *This is the first letter I've got from a 'girl' I like.*

He read through it again as he considered whether to text or email or call Martie, or maybe just write a letter. When Martie sent the letter to Jefferson, she had no idea when he would receive it. But there was the hope it would prompt a response from him.

Jeff pondered which kind of communication to use. The letter had been a surprise, a wonderful one that convinced him she felt the same as him. *Maybe she would like to get one from me. I will send one, but I want to hear her voice.*

Deciding she couldn't know how long it would take for her letter to be delivered to him, Jeff called her, thinking, *I won't tell her I received the letter unless she asks me about it.*

"Hello."

"Hello to you. It's Jeff—Jefferson."

"Yes, I see."

Jefferson said, "Don't know why we've stopped keeping in touch. I've missed your texts and calls, emails, too."

"So have I." *He said nothing about a letter, must not have got it yet.*

"How have you been?" Jefferson asked. "Anything exciting happening in Nebraska?"

Martie told him, "No. We've had a lot of snow and it's cold. How about you? Any new adventures?"

"I did go to the meeting of the Overland Park Historical Society. Not an adventure, but good to see everyone," Jeff told her, still wondering about the woman who had sat down beside him. "We had one bad snowstorm, but otherwise, it's been warmer than usual. Some experts say that could be bad for the fruit trees. Apparently, they need so much cold to produce a good crop."

"I never heard that," Martie told him.

"Well, I never had either," Jefferson agreed. "Guess I don't really have any news. Good to talk to you. I need to call Jerilyn too. You probably know all that's going on with her."

"I probably do. She and Josh stay busy with school. I'm glad to talk to you too."

Though he had no more to say, Jeff was loath to say goodbye but did, adding, "I'll try to stay in touch more."

Martie said, "Me too. Bye." She was still wondering about the letter she had sent and what Jefferson might think when he received it.

Dear Martie,

I received your letter before I called you. It meant so much to me—showing me that you cared the same as I do.

Was glad for the phone call, too—though I like the idea of a letter, unexpected but special. I can hold the words and read them whenever.

Maybe I will plan a trip to visit Jerilyn and Josh.

Love,

Jefferson

Jeff checked the return label from the envelope that had held the letter from Martie and copied it onto the one where he had already written her name. When he added his return label, he thought, *She has been at this address, but I haven't been at hers in Nebraska. If I ever am, what might it be like?* He remembered some of the awkward times that week she, Josh, and Jerilyn had stayed for Christmas.

According to the postmark, he determined it had taken five days for Martie's letter to reach him, wondering how long it would be before she received his. He needed stamps, so it would be the next day before it would be on its way.

~

Jon was spending a bit more time with his dad. Linda had left the day before New Year's and would be gone longer than any time since the two got together. He had told her he would like to know how his dad really felt about Martie Wilson.

Linda asked, "Would it bother you if he wanted to be with her?"

He wondered why she asked and she said, "Because of your mother."

Jon had stayed quiet, his mind returning to that time of his mother's death and all the years before. There was no question that his parents were deeply in love—then how heartbroken his dad was when she died and how much he had missed her.

Jon shared that with Linda, then added he knew there was no question that his dad had liked Martie from the first time they met, saying, "I'm pretty sure he hadn't felt that way about anyone else since Mom died. Now, realizing I'm in love with you and want to be with you, I can understand his feelings."

Jeff smiled, knowing Jon had questions, but they didn't come up in a regular conversation. He would answer them when he was ready, knowing the same as everyone else—he and Martie lived hundreds of miles apart. Instead, he asked Jon, "How are you and Linda getting along? Any future plans?"

But thinking about Martie, Jeff recalled that when he was with her, few as the times had been, there was that extra beat of his heart surprising him. He had been so much in love with Joyce all the years they were married, not expecting to love again.

When he mailed the letter to Martie, Jeff wondered what his son might think of that. He still had asked no questions—nor had Jack. Jerilyn probably had questions too—for both him and

Martie—Mattie to her. Had she approached her mother-in-law with them? Perhaps not, thinking Martie would have told him.

Ah, Martie, what are we to do? Are there any weddings planned, inviting us, giving us opportunity to be together again? It's only a few weeks before Valentine's Day. Maybe there will at least be a proposal.

In Nebraska, Martie was also thinking about Valentine's Day, considering whether to send one to Jefferson. *Maybe I'll wait, see if he might send a letter to me before doing so.*

~

Mitchell's sister had her baby, and he drove into Scottsbluff to see her, stopping first to get Nancy. He was wearing the "Uncle Mitchell" shirt Sandy and Ronnie had given him for Christmas, so she changed into the one they had given her with her name on it.

When Mitch took her home after the visit to the hospital, he reminded her, "Don't forget to ring the bell." It was the gift he had given her for Christmas, "to ring when you need me."

Nancy wondered how it could make a difference, but she hadn't been ringing it. Maybe doing so would at least help her feel closer to him.

Fourteen

In Overland Park, Kansas, Jonson Tate was changing the calendar to February, making note of Valentine's Day. Linda would still be away, but he thought, *Should I get a gift for her anyway?* He remembered seeing engagement and wedding rings when he got the bracelet he had given her for Christmas.

Is it too soon to think about that possibility—marriage? Jack and Jayden are married, and they got together after Linda and I did. But they were always together, not separated like Linda and I often are.

A few days later, Jon noticed his dad staring at the calendar. Was Jeff thinking about Valentine's Day? Maybe sending a card to Martie? He didn't know that the two had written letters to each other but was aware of the occasional email, text, or phone call.

And Jeff was considering doing so. Even the grocery store had a card section, along with possible gifts, gift bags, and wrapping paper. When the valentines appeared, he surreptitiously checked them out, reading the words, pondering how Martie might feel if she got one from him. If he chose one, what might the checker think when they swiped it? He had never used self-checkout. Maybe he could try it with only the valentine.

When Martie received the letter from Jefferson, she did the same as he had done. There had been emails in between, but now she called.

"I got your letter."

"Good."

"So are you planning to come for a visit?" she asked, referring to the words he had written.

Jeff said, "I could—maybe I should. Miss seeing Jerilyn." At her silence, he added, "You too."

"And I miss seeing you," Martie told him. "How can that be? We barely know each other."

It was awhile before Jeff agreed, "Yes."

~

For several weeks, Nancy and Mitchell had been attending three churches, one Sunday at her home church in Plattsford, one Sunday at the church in Scottsbluff, and one Sunday at Mt. Olive, the home church of the Robbins family.

Nancy had already been thinking she should spend more time with her mother, and one way to do that was to drive in to Plattsford to church more often. Besides, loving Mitchell and knowing he loved her, hopefully there would soon be a wedding, and she would want that to be at her home church. With that in mind, she spoke to the congregation in Scottsbluff.

"There have been changes in my life, and I want to spend more time with my mother. Part of that will be going to church with her in Plattsford, so this will be my last regular Sunday with you. I have so enjoyed worshipping with you; thank you for being a refuge for me."

She was crying by the time she finished, so Mitchell went to stand with her. They would be driving in to have a meal with her mother, but nearly everyone in attendance wanted to hug her and wish her happiness. That delayed them enough that Mitchell called Mattie to let her know they would be late.

Nancy had no idea that Mitchell had in mind to propose but wanted to speak to Mattie first, asking permission to do so. When they got to her house, Josh and Jerilyn were there and he asked them to occupy Nancy for a while. Mattie was more than happy to give her permission. She hugged Mitchell and told him, "I love you too."

There had been no more letters between Jeff and Martie, but they were again keeping in touch often with texts, emails, and calls. As soon as all the young people had left on Sunday, Martie sent a text to Jeff, telling him about Mitchell's petition.

Instead of texting back, Jeff called and asked, "When is the proposal going to be?"

"He didn't say when he was going to ask her, and it's apparent Nancy has no clue. Anyway, you and I were wondering if there would be any weddings or proposals."

"Except often, there's a lot of time between proposals and weddings," Jeff reminded her.

"That's true, but our kids haven't waited long once they knew they wanted to be married," Martie said.

"Yeah. I'll be waiting to hear. But then, I might not be invited," Jeff added, sounding sad.

After their conversation, Jefferson and Martie each thought again about valentines and that special day getting closer. Just as he was contemplating sending one to her, Martie was pondering choosing one for Jefferson. Each wondered if they could even find one with the right words, words that would hint at how they felt about the other without being specific.

~

It was Valentine's Day, and Nancy was dejected when she picked up the list of those needing treatment. She had told Sara the day before that she wasn't expecting anything special. Mitchell had said nothing about the day. Maybe he hadn't paid any attention to the calendar, but there were even ads on TV featuring jewelry, or candies, or suggestions for special dates.

A beautiful bouquet of roses interspersed with baby's breath was delivered to the appointment desk mid-morning. *I wonder who they're for*, Nancy thought, trying to guess as she looked around the room, having convinced herself they wouldn't be for her.

Then Kaye at the desk motioned, indicating they were. She removed the card and read, "Love you so much. Have you rung the bell today?" Nancy hadn't but seeing that everyone in the room had their eyes on her, she raised it and rang it with a happy smile.

Almost immediately, there was a call from Mitchell. He said, "We were talking about that new restaurant. How about going there tonight?"

A time was set, and he told her, "Dress up."

~

When they returned to her house, Nancy brought the special valentine she had bought for him to Mitchell. He read it and told her, "It's perfect!"

They were sitting on the couch and, with the valentine still in his hand, he leaned over to kiss her. Then he was on his knee in front of her, telling her how much he loved her. "I had no idea it was possible to love another person like I love you. I want you to be mine for always. I asked your mother for permission, so now I'm asking you, Nancy Elizabeth Wilson. Will you marry me and love me for the rest of our lives?"

She hadn't expected that and was crying when she leaned over to give him a kiss. Both ended up on the floor, wrapped in each other's arms. Then Nancy realized she hadn't given an answer to Mitchell and said, "Oh, yes, forever!"

The ring he put on her finger was one that came from his great grandparents. It was the patterned handle of a silver spoon fashioned into a ring. Mitchell's grandfather had given it to his grandmother, then his father, Dennis, had given it to Meg.

"It was sort of a promise ring until they chose their permanent ones. I hope you will wear it until we have time to shop for one."

Nancy loved it, and though there was no gem, everyone at work the next day noticed it immediately and congratulated her.

~

Nancy called her mother after Mitchell left, though it was later than she usually would have. "Mom, Mitchell proposed. He told me he had asked you for permission, so I know it's no surprise to you. Of course, I said, 'yes'."

"Oh, Nancy! I'm so happy for you. There's no question of the love between you. Any idea when there might be a wedding?"

"No. And, no, I have no ideas. I bet you do," said with an obvious smile.

"Well, no. You will have to decide for yourselves, but you know I'm happy about this too. Both of my kids have their love."

～

After talking to Nancy, Martie looked again at the valentine she had received from Jefferson. She was holding it while she was talking to her daughter.

The printed words on the card read, "I'm sending this Valentine so I can say you're special in every way." Jeff had added a few more words. "And you're special to me. Best wishes for your happiness every day." Followed by "Love, Jefferson."

Martie had sent one to him with similar words, those printed on the card as well as the personal ones she had added.

There was no other communication between them on that special day. It was as if they were purposely waiting, examining again the feelings that had begun at Josh and Jerilyn's wedding then became stronger when Martie stayed a week at Jefferson's home after Jack's and Jayden's wedding. When Martie opened the card and read the words, there was a leap of her heart, as well as a special feeling reaching into her stomach, that she had no answer for.

The only other person she had felt so strongly for was Andrew. She had not expected to love again. The words in the valentine from Jefferson reminded her of those times with him and their wondering if there might be other weddings where they could be together. But though the feelings were there, what could come of it? They were still so many miles apart. Why had the valentine and its words generated this need to again explore those feelings?

Smiling, she thought about her daughter's engagement. No date set for a wedding, but maybe there would be another one, another time to be with Jefferson. She would like to talk to him, but it was late for her and an hour later for him. She decided, *I'll send an email. Maybe he will call when he gets it*, expecting it would be the next day.

Dear Jefferson,

I received the valentine you sent—today, this special day. Wondering if you got mine. Seems like we can only hope that mail is delivered when we want it to be. I love the words in the card as well as the ones you added. You wondered when Mitchell would propose. Nancy called a few minutes ago to let me know he did— tonight. A special Valentine for her. Perhaps there will be another wedding when we can be together.

Love,

Martie

Jeff had received the valentine from Martie and just as she had done, read it more than once. He would like to talk to her, but decided, *I'll wait till tomorrow.* When he got her email, he considered not waiting to do so, but checked the time and thought, *Tomorrow will be better.*

~

It was early, but Jeff had been awake for some time, recalling the words of the valentine he had received from Martie, and thinking of the news she had sent in an email.

Nancy and Mitchell were now engaged, though that didn't necessarily mean their wedding would be soon. Strange—why were they thinking only of their children's weddings as times they could be together? *But how can we change that? Do we want to? Our relationship—if there is one—has certainly not been normal. But every time I see her, no matter how long it has been, I feel that flutter again that I felt at Jerilyn's wedding. And there's no question, Martie felt something too. Was it as strong as what I experienced each of those times?*

~

Checking the time, Jeff thought he should get up. It wasn't normal for him to lay in bed pondering and remembering. It was too early to call Martie, but he needed to have breakfast. There was still some of the Maple Bacon coffee she had given him for Christmas, so first thing was to start a pot.

There was bacon and toast and a glass of orange juice to go with it. While he was preparing everything, Jon walked in, home from his latest shift.

"Hey, Dad. Looks like you're having a late breakfast. Everything okay?"

Jeff had brought the valentine to the kitchen, and it was on the table in its envelope. Jon picked it up, noted the return address, then asked his dad, "Is it a valentine?"

Jeff's back was to him, so Jon missed the slight blush and secret smile. Turning back to his son, Jeff said, "Yes, a late breakfast, everything's okay, and it's a valentine from Martie.

"Are you hungry? I can fry more bacon."

Jon assured him, "I ate already, but if it's okay, I'll join you anyway so we can catch up on what's happening."

He had retrieved a cup from the cabinet and added, "I will have coffee."

Fifteen

When they were both sitting at the table, Jon asked, "So did you send a valentine to Martie?"

His dad swallowed his bite of toast and took a sip of coffee before he answered.

"Yes. We've been sending letters occasionally."

"Linda and I do too when she's gone for a while, though she doesn't get mine until she's home."

"She sent an email last night," Jeff continued. "Nancy and Mitchell are engaged. Looking at his watch, he added, "I'm going to call her in a few minutes, see what else she might know."

He could tell that the news about the engagement affected his son and wondered what might be going through his mind. Did he have any thoughts about him and Linda getting married some day?

~

In Plattsford, Nebraska, Martie Wilson had been up and around for a while, earlier than usual. She was disappointed that she hadn't heard from Jefferson, having hoped for a call, but there had not even been a text or email.

Thinking about Nancy now being engaged, she had brought the calendar to the table. No idea when a wedding might occur, but she wanted to check dates anyway, knowing it wasn't up to her to make suggestions. Though she was remembering there had been a very short time between Josh and Jerilyn's engagement and the day they married. The same had been true of Jerilyn's brother Jack.

She had to admit that she hoped for that same timeline for Nancy and Mitchell. But was it because there would be another wedding, perhaps an opportunity to see Jefferson again? There was not even an assurance that he would be invited.

His daughter is now living in the same town I am. Maybe I should just look forward to a time Jefferson might come to visit Jerilyn.

~

Jeff noticed that though he had mentioned calling Martie, it seemed Jon wanted to stay with him. So he took time to send her a text. *"Planned to call, then Jon came in—seems like he needs something. Will call soon, so much to talk about. :heart emoji:"*

He stayed silent for a while after sending it, then asked Jon, "Something you want to talk about?"

"Huh? Why do you ask that?"

"The news about the engagement seemed to affect you—but maybe you're pondering something else?" Jeff asked.

"Maybe," Jon admitted. "Linda has been gone longer than any other time since we've been together. We keep in touch, but I'd sure like to be able to hold her. Guess I'm jealous when I know other couples can be together."

"I know what you mean," his dad agreed. "Now I need to call Martie."

Jon grinned as he left the room. Sure sounded like his dad had special feelings for Martie. And they were separated too.

~

Martie was happy when she received Jefferson's text telling her he would be calling. She wondered what Jon's anxiety might be, and how long she would have to wait, trying to remember when they last talked.

Just as she finished that thought, there was the sound signaling a call. She felt the leap of her heart, knowing she was going to hear Jefferson's voice.

"Hello."

"Sorry I couldn't call sooner," Jeff said.

"It's okay. I understand. Were you able to take care of whatever Jon needed?"

Jeff had also experienced that special feeling that washed over him every time he heard Martie's voice. *But what might come of it? Maybe this is the most it will ever be.*

"I guess as much as I could. Linda has been away on flights for a long time, the longest since they've been together. And he's missing her, jealous of those who can be together. I sure understand that."

Martie agreed, "So do I."

Both were quiet after those revealing words, then Martie asked, "So will Linda be home soon?"

"Don't know. He didn't say and I didn't ask. Enough about that, what about Nancy and Mitchell?"

"Believe it or not, Nancy was surprised. There had been no hint from Mitchell that he was even aware of Valentine's Day."

Jeff said, "Guess that could almost be considered normal for us men."

"Maybe," Martie agreed. "Anyway, he called her at work, mentioned a new restaurant in Scottsbluff, told her to dress up. They enjoyed their meal. When they got back to her house, she gave him a valentine, then he proposed.

"Mitchell gave her a special ring that his grandfather had given to his grandmother, then Mitchell's father had given to his mother. They'll choose a diamond ring later."

Jeff said, "Sounds romantic."

"Yes," from Martie.

No more words from either of them for a while. During their conversation, both were remembering the last time they had seen each other—Christmas in Overland Park, and their hug just before she left with Josh and Jerilyn.

Jeff thought, *I had no idea how much I missed having hugs from someone I love—a different feeling from hugs with a child.* Then, *do I love her?*

Martie asked, "Anything interesting happening in Overland Park, Kansas?"

"Can't think of anything. How about Plattsford, Nebraska?"

"Same here. Oh, have I mentioned that Mitchell's sister had her baby? She's already almost a month old."

"She. So it's a girl?"

"Yes. They named her Bethany Robin. And you can't miss how enthused Mitchell is about being Uncle Mitchell. Makes me wonder how he would feel about being a daddy."

~

Jon had taken a nap after the words with his father. When he woke, his thoughts returned to those earlier ones about a possible relationship between his dad and Josh's mother. Was there a growing love between them? Sure seemed to be from what he had observed.

How do I feel about that? But what could happen anyway? They have only been together at weddings. Well, there was that week after Jack's wedding.

Linda, how I would love to be together with you, to hug you, to kiss you. And a letter would be good, haven't had one for a while. I'll write one to you, though you won't get it till you're home, but I can tell you how I feel, how I miss you, how I love you.

Things had been slow, but Jon was surprised how much time had passed since he and Linda were together. Then, as if in answer to his prayers, there was a letter from her.

Jeff had told Martie that nothing special was happening in OP, but he had been more active in recent weeks with the Overland Park Historical Society. He probably hadn't mentioned it because it had been a regular part of his life in the past and he was just returning to it.

Currently, Jeff was volunteering at their office on Thursday afternoons. Sometimes they were busy, others, not so much, but it was good to get caught up on what was happening with the Society. He was realizing that with Jack married and no longer in the house and Jon's shifts keeping him away, he needed more interaction with others. His time at OPHS was providing that.

The woman he had seen a couple of times at the grocery store who had asked him about his kids' weddings was one of the others who spent time there, though not always on Thursdays. Jeff learned that her name was Sheila Massey, but didn't recognize that her manner around him was almost flirtatious.

~

Before she was engaged, but after Mitch told her he loved her, Nancy had been driving to Plattsford to go to church with her mother. Mitchell occasionally drove in from the ranch to take her. Mattie was glad for that as it gave her opportunities to learn more about him and get better acquainted with the man who was going to be her son-in-law. Then she thought, *It would be good to get acquainted with his family, too.*

The next Sunday that Mitchell took Nancy to church in Plattsford, then to Mattie's for lunch, she broached the subject with both of them. "I've so enjoyed getting to know Mitchell better. Don't know why I hadn't thought about it before, but I would like to get to know his family too. It's not like they live in a different state."

She smiled, as did Nancy, when she continued. "I didn't know Jerilyn's family until the wedding. But they live in a different state, and there are hundreds of miles between here and Overland Park, Kansas." Wondering as she said it, *Would I feel differently about Jefferson if I had met him before?*

Nancy and Mitchell agreed that it would be a good thing. Mattie suggested, "Maybe you two can talk about it, come up with an idea. Knowing all that goes on with a ranch, I'm not sure what would be best—when, where, what, everything. I would be glad to have you all come here."

Mitchell said, "I like the idea. I'll check with Dad and Mom on a possible date, probably a weekend. But I do have a thought. When we decide," turning to Mattie, he asked, "how about you drive in to Nancy's on a Saturday, spend the night with her. Then I'll drive in on Sunday morning, pick you both up, and go back to the ranch. We could make it early enough to go to church at Mt. Olive."

"That sounds good," Nancy said, then to her mother, "so what else is going on in your life? Anything exciting, interesting?"

Mattie pondered her question later. *The only thing exciting and interesting to me is the communication I have with Jefferson, but I'm not ready to share that.*

She had no idea that both Nancy and Jerilyn had noted at least some of that and were aware there was a special connection between their parents but didn't quite know what to do about it. And neither of the daughters was ready to ask any questions.

Sixteen

artie had told Jefferson about the plan to visit the Rocking R, mostly to get acquainted with Mitchell's family. She called him the day after to tell him about the experience.

"Martie." When Jeff answered, it was almost with a question in his voice.

"Yes. You sound surprised to hear from me."

"I am, kind of," he said. "It's Monday morning, beginning of the week. We usually talk later in the day, later in the week."

Martie asked, "Do we? Sounds like you're keeping score."

"Maybe I am," Jeff admitted. "Always glad to hear your voice, wondering when we'll talk again. Is there a reason for this call?"

"Does there have to be a reason?" Martie was enjoying the back-and-forth word play; it was almost teasing.

Jefferson said, "Guess not. I know occasionally I call just because I want to hear your voice."

After that admission, there was a short pause before Martie told him, "So do I. But there is a reason this time.

"We had talked about the plan to go to the Robbins' ranch."

"Yeah, I remember."

"It was yesterday."

"Ah," Jeff said. "So much to talk about. Was it a good day? Did you enjoy it? Did you like them?"

Martie started laughing.

"What?"

"All those questions," Martie answered. "I wouldn't have expected them from you."

"Oh, sorry."

"No worry," Martie told him. "Don't remember if I told you Mitchell was going to pick us up at Nancy's. Anyway, I drove to her place Saturday afternoon. She and I had a wonderful visit, more time together with just us than we usually have. We always ask ourselves, 'Why'."

Jeff agreed. "I know how that is. With Jerilyn in Nebraska now, and Jack out of the house, Jon and I say we need to spend more time together, but it rarely happens."

Martie continued with her report about the day with the Robbins family. "On our way to church, Mitchell talked about how he felt after his first therapy with Nancy. He had never shared it with her, and I could tell she was affected. There were tears in her eyes.

"He had told Nancy that his folks knew he loved her before he did. That was partly from what they observed when he told them about his therapist. Then he told me that Nancy was the first to say I love you.

"That's when I told Mitchell that I had advised her to tell him if she did.

"Nancy said, 'Yes, and I regretted it as soon as I said it.'

"Mitchell reached for her hand, kissed it, and said, 'I was so glad to hear it.'

"Nancy said she wondered if she would have to be the one to propose, then decided she wouldn't, even if they spent the rest of their lives with Mitchell in therapy.

"All of Mitchell's family were waiting for us at the church and we sat together."

Jeff asked, "Did you like them?"

"I do. But I expected to. I love Mitchell, and they have all been good to Nancy. No question they love her. And the baby! Bethany is so sweet; it would be easy to spoil her. I told Dennis and Meg I was jealous, wondering if I will ever be a grandmother."

There was a pause, since Jefferson, too, was anxious to have grandchildren.

"I guess you went to the ranch after church?"

"Yes."

"Did it bring back memories?" Jeff asked.

"To an extent. Those days for me seem so far in the past. Dennis asked if I would like to take a tour of the property. And I would—told him so—but I'm expecting there will be many times in the future that I can do so. Might even want to ride.

"We can talk about yesterday another time. Do you have any plans for the week?"

"There's the usual trip to the grocery store," Jeff told her. "Doesn't that sound exciting? I will be at OPHS Thursday afternoon. They'll soon start making plans for summer activities. I'll have to decide how much I want to be involved. What about you?"

Martie said, "I may start work in the flower beds. It's getting warmer, and there is some cleaning that needs to be done before I think of adding anything new."

"That would be on Joyce's mind if she was here. I remember how excited she would get planning for the new season.

"One year, the church sponsored a Benefit Garden Tour—ours, well hers—was one of the featured ones. She potted up a lot of plants to sell to anyone who might be interested. There was even an article with pictures in the newspaper. And some of those who visited the garden sent letters later expressing their enjoyment of the day."

Martie could almost feel Jefferson's heartache as he remembered those times. And how she understood.

"Sorry. Memories sometimes creep up on me."

Martie assured him, "How well I know."

Jefferson continued, "Have enjoyed talking to you, learning what's happening in your life. Guess there's still no idea when there might be a wedding?"

"No," Martie told him, "but I'm thinking it's not going to be a long engagement."

"That's good, not that it's any of my business," Jefferson said.

"I feel the same. Now, guess I better say bye and get to whatever I decide to do with the day. So, bye."

"Bye to you too. Don't get sunburned."

Jeff held his phone for a while before putting it in his pocket, pondering all they had talked about, wondering if the feelings between him and Martie might have been different if they had known each other before Josh and Jerilyn's wedding.

His thoughts returned to the time he first met Josh and realized how much he meant to Jerilyn. She was concerned about the hundreds of miles between them, believing their relationship could never be more than a long-distance friendship. He had told her it didn't have to be that way. "If you figure out you love each other, you'll figure out how to solve the problem."

That was easy to point out to Jerilyn, but is the answer the same for Martie and me? Are our feelings the beginning of love—or just a strong like? Well, I said I needed to get groceries, but I need to make a list first.

Jeff started the list with Sunflower Seed bread. Joyce had picked it up more out of curiosity than anything else many years ago. It had become a favorite of all of them, and, since that first time, it was about the only bread they bought. It made wonderful grilled cheese sandwiches that they made often.

Jeff had filled the cart with everything on his list, then checked around to see if there might be something he had forgotten. As he entered the line to the checkout he heard, "Jeff."

He looked toward the person in front of him and saw the woman from OPHS, trying to remember her name, Oh yeah, "Sheila."

She continued with, "We seem to often do our shopping at the same time."

"I guess."

Naming an upcoming event, she asked, "Are you planning to go?"

He hadn't decided yet, though he probably would, but told her, "Not sure."

Anyone else could have recognized that the woman was almost flirting, obviously interested in a relationship with Jeff. And she had not seen him give any special attention to any lady who might be around. If Jeff noticed, he chose to ignore it. If he developed a meaningful relationship, he wanted it to be with Martie.

Sheila wasn't ready to give up yet; her eye had been on Jeff Tate for a long time. "So, any more weddings planned? Seems like there have been several in your family in recent months."

She was confused when Jeff told her, "There is a new engagement—my son-in-law's sister."

"Oh, here?"

"No. In Nebraska." Picking up his bagged groceries, he said, "Good talking to you."

Seventeen

Jon remembered that his dad's birthday was coming up. Though they had not done so in the past, he thought it would be good if he and Jack planned something to celebrate with him.

Jon knew he would be off that day and thought, *I'll check with Jack, see what his schedule is before talking to Dad about it.*

Jack was surprised when he got the text from his brother reminding him of their dad's birthday and suggesting the three do something special. As it happened, he was also off, so any celebration could take place on that day, unless Jeff already had plans.

Jon's next step was to present the idea to his dad, so a few days before his birthday, he told Jeff about the plan while they were having breakfast.

"Dad, your birthday is coming up next week."

"So it is."

"Jack and I want to spend the day with you. Is there someplace we can take you? Maybe a place you haven't visited for a while, then out to eat after."

Jeff didn't say anything, then Jon noticed there were tears in his eyes. "Dad?"

Jeff assured him he would love spending the day with the boys. "Can't remember a time we've ever done so.

"And as a matter of fact, there is a place I've been wanting to visit recently. There have been some changes and additions there, but I don't want to go alone. It's the World War I Memorial. You know, when it first opened way back in 1920, they called it Liberty Memorial; that's what it was for a long time. Would be good to share the experience with my sons."

The museum holds a world-class collection in the heart of America, with a permanent exhibition in the main gallery—The World War 1914–1919, a view of the world war through the eyes of those who lived it.

Some of the other exhibits, which caught the attention of the men, included the Choctaw Code Talkers, a forgotten story of that war. They also noted The Little War about the lives of children who were swept up by the storm of the war while adults were fighting on the front line or supporting the war effort.

Jon and Jack wanted to take their dad for a meal afterward, and he chose the Dragon Inn. As they enjoyed the food, there was much conversation about what they had seen at the museum, much more than they had expected.

Jon said, "You know we still didn't see everything, need to go back another time."

"That's for sure," Jack agreed.

Jeff smiled, happy to see the interest of his sons.

When Jayden learned of the plans for the day and that it was her father-in-law's birthday, she told Jack she would make a cake and bring it to the house when they returned. He had told neither his dad nor his brother, so it was a sweet surprise. Jayden had learned how old he was and included numbered candles. She lit them, the three young people sang "Happy Birthday," then Jeff blew them out.

"It's been a great day. Maybe the best birthday I've had for a long time. Thank you all."

Just as he finished that thought, he had a call from his daughter. "Jerilyn."

"Happy Birthday, Dad. Have you done anything exciting?"

Her brothers, realizing it was their sister on the phone, said, "Hi, Jerilyn!"

"Ah, the boys are there."

"Yes, and Jayden. It's been quite a day. Jack, Jon, and I visited the World War I Museum, then went to Dragon Inn to eat. Jayden brought a birthday cake after we were back here."

"So, a good day. I'm glad. I knew a little bit about it because Jayden called to ask how old you were going to be and what your favorite cake was."

"Yes, special. How are things in Nebraska?"

Jerilyn said, "Maybe you know Nancy and Mitch have set a wedding date?"

"Yes."

"If you haven't already, I'm sure you will get an invitation," she told him. "I'll let you go now so you can enjoy the rest of your day. Love you."

"I love you too. Hi to Josh."

After the call ended, Jayden told Jeff that everyone at church had said to tell him Happy Birthday. Jeff hadn't told Jerilyn that he had already received the wedding invitation, but now, after a little more conversation and discussion about this special day, he told them, "Martie's daughter—Josh's sister—is getting married in a few weeks. I just got an invitation. Do you think I should go?"

Jack had no idea why his father would want to go. He had not been there after his and Jayden's wedding when Martie spent a week—the week before Christmas—with Jeff, along with Jerilyn and Josh. But Jon was and remembered the attention his dad had given Martie. And he recalled the question Linda had asked, "Would it bother you if he would want to be with her?"

Jayden told Jeff, "Of course." Her sister Carly was dating Mitchell's cousin, so she also knew about the upcoming wedding.

Jack asked, if he went, would he drive or fly.

His dad told them, "For the wedding, I would probably fly. Maybe drive another time."

Jack was still perplexed, and they all made note of the words 'another time.'

~

Jerilyn had told Martie earlier that it was her dad's birthday. She considered calling him but didn't want to interrupt a possible celebration. Instead, she sent an email wishing him a 'Happy Birthday,' hoping he might call.

Later in the day, Jack and Jayden had left and Jon retreated to his room, wanting to contact Linda and tell her about the day. Jeff saw Martie's email. His heart began beating faster as it often did just thinking about that woman—so far away in Nebraska.

As Martie hoped, though she hadn't suggested it, Jeff did call. He wanted to hear her voice, feel like she had been, was, part of the day.

Jon had told Linda of the plans for the birthday celebration, and just as Jayden had, she thought it was a sweet plan. So after his brother and sister-in-law left, he sent a text to Linda about the day, telling her Jayden had brought a cake to the house. *Wish you could have been here, too.*

Even as he sent the text, other thoughts were floating around in his mind. Before they left, with the thought of another upcoming wedding, Jayden had asked how things were with Jon and Linda. "Do you have a date in mind?"

"For what?"

"A wedding."

He told her things were great, "But we're not even engaged, sure haven't talked about marriage."

Jack told his brother, "I've been wondering too. You and Linda were together before Jayden and I were. And we've been married almost four months."

Both Jayden and Jack apologized and admitted it wasn't any of their business. But they were so happy together, wanting the same thing for the other couple. Jayden gave him a hug and said, "You will know when the time is right."

Jeff had kept quiet during the discussion, though his attention had moved from one to the other of his sons. But he could tell the thoughts they had voiced were settled in Jon's mind.

Jeff's call to Martie had ended when Jon came out of his room, his mind still on the earlier conversations with his brother and sister-in-law.

"What do you think, Dad?" he asked.

"About?"

"Me getting married—or at least engaged."

Though he hadn't expressed any opinions during the discussion about a possible wedding, he wondered if Jon would have more to say. Now he told his son, "That's up to you and Linda. But I know you love each other, and marriage, or at least an engagement, would be a natural progression."

As those words were settling, Jeff asked, "Have you thought about whether you will ask her parents for their blessing?"

"Well, no." After giving the idea time to settle into his mind, Jon smiled and said, "Thanks, Dad. That would be a good beginning."

Eighteen

*J*eff couldn't stop smiling. He wanted to call Martie and tell her this latest news—perhaps another wedding—at least an engagement. *Guess I better wait until something actually happens. For now, I can look forward to Nancy's wedding in a few weeks. I will see Martie then, and of course, Jerilyn.*

Martie had said she could hardly believe that both of her children would be married in a fairly short time. Now Jeff could say the same. Well, if Jon got engaged. Though that didn't mean he would get married soon. He and Linda had been together—dating more than a year. Maybe an engagement would last that long.

~

Jeff was missing his usual day at OPHS. He had no idea that Sheila stopped by often, hoping to see him. But though it was a bit late in the year, after much work with spade and hoe and rake, he had finally restored one of Joyce's flower beds. Some flowers were even coming up. *Well, I think they're flowers. Don't look like any weeds I'm familiar with. I need to water them, maybe go to Family Tree to get some more to fill in the bare spots.*

In Nebraska, all of Martie's flower beds were flourishing, maybe not as advanced as Jeff's was, since it was a bit farther north. She had also helped Jerilyn with her first bed. The place had actually been chosen in the fall when they planted the bulbs Jerilyn had received at her bridal shower. They had already enjoyed the first blooms from the garden. Josh had done all the digging then and in the spring as they expanded the area, making room to plant the seeds her friends had given to her.

As soon as they felt all was ready, they chose a place for the stone Jerilyn had received at her bridal shower. It was heart-shaped with their names on it, Josh and Jerilyn Wilson, the date of their wedding, and the words, Happily Ever After.

Martie had led Jerilyn and Josh on a tour of her yard, checking out all the beds and pointing out some plants that would be good starts for theirs. Josh was carrying a spade, and Jerilyn was pulling a wagon, which held the plants as they were dug up. The wagon had been Josh's, and his mother had learned years ago it was a perfect vehicle for carrying any plants to be moved to a new home.

Jerilyn told Josh, "Maybe we need to get a wagon to use at home."

"Okay," he agreed.

When they had chosen what they wanted, Jerilyn pulled the wagon to Josh's pickup. They removed a cardboard box they had brought and transferred the plants to it. When they got home, they would place them in a shady place, waiting for the next day when they would go into their new home.

When she was planning the garden, Jerilyn had told everyone she would call it Joyce's Garden in honor of her mother. Now she wondered if there might be someone who could create a sign she could place among the flowers.

~

In Overland Park, Jon had been surprised at his dad's birthday event when everyone had asked him about his plans for the future with Linda. But it took little time for him to take Jeff's advice about asking her parents' permission to propose, wondering why he hadn't already considered it. Linda would be back in Overland Park in a couple of days, and he hoped he could get that permission before she was home, not wanting to waste any more time.

Richard and Donna were happy to give their permission, knowing their daughter was in love with Jonson Tate and there was no question that he loved her too. They had no doubt he would be a wonderful son-in-law. When Linda returned home, they were anxious for the proposal to take place and had to be careful about any conversation they had with their daughter so they wouldn't give anything away.

Linda returned home sooner than Jon expected and surprised him at the station. They had a short time to visit before there was an alarm and he had to leave. There had been time to mention a possible date, returning to the park where they went on their first one.

When they got there, they went first to the town, then the swings. When they reached them, Jon asked Linda if she wanted to go up again. She did and chose one with a bit higher seat than that first time and told him, "Okay, I'm ready."

Instead of pushing her, he got down on one knee in front of her and took her hand. After the initial surprise, there were tears in her eyes. There was no question about their love for each other and her answer to his proposal. After their first kiss as an engaged couple, Jon asked if she wanted to see more of the park or head home. She told him she wanted to be pushed on the swing first, the perfect conclusion to a perfect day.

When they got to the Morgans', Linda's parents were anxious to hear about the day. When she told them they were engaged, Donna and Richard wrapped their arms around both of them for a hug and said, "Wonderful! Congratulations!"

On his way home, Jon thought he needed to tell his dad. Jeff was watching the news when his son walked in, went to his dad, and hugged him, telling him, "This has been a very special day and I need to thank you."

"Oh?"

"Yeah, on your birthday, you pushed me to talk to Linda's parents, get their permission to propose to her. You are looking at a happy, engaged man."

"Congratulations! Any idea when there might be a wedding?"

"No. But we're going shopping for an engagement ring tomorrow."

Jeff thought, *So maybe another wedding when I get to see Martie,* then realized, *Maybe not. Though Jerilyn and Josh would probably come, that doesn't mean she would.*

It was bedtime, and Jeff headed for his room with the realization that all of his and Joyce's kids had found their special forever one. Believing that God is involved in all aspects of our life, he prayed, "Thank you, God, for being with them, leading them to the one who will complete their life as you did me and Joyce. Be with me, help me to always be a good father, counselor, and advisor, as they might need without interfering. Amen."

~

With all that was on his mind, dreams invaded Jeff's sleep. It was a summer day, a day off for him. He and Joyce and their kids were debating what to do to occupy the time. The kids wanted to go to

Worlds of Fun. He glanced at his wife and saw the sweet smile that had caught his attention those years ago when they had first met. It still affected him the same—an increased heartbeat and a desire to kiss those lips. They were standing together, and he leaned down to do just that.

His daughter and sons looked at each other, shaking their heads. After the kiss, Jeff and Joyce looked at them and smiled. They loved them so much. They were all good kids, making them proud and happy for their family.

The scene changed. The kids were older, and Joyce was fading away as Jeff reached toward her. He woke with tears in his eyes. "Oh, Joyce. How I wish you were here with me and the kids, grateful, as I am, for their special one."

He remembered his earlier thought to call Martie about another possible engagement. With the memory of his dreams, he sent an email instead.

You may have already learned that Jon and Linda are engaged. No idea of a wedding date. I would never have expected that all of my kids would have found their special one in what seems like a short time to me.

〜

There was little time between Jon's engagement and Jeff's trip to Nebraska for Nancy Wilson's wedding. Both Josh and Jerilyn picked him up at the airport when he arrived, the day before the rehearsal.

Jerilyn hugged him and said, "Dad, so good to see you."

Hugging her back, Jeff said, "You too. Didn't know I would miss you like I have."

Josh asked if he had checked any luggage.

"Yeah," Jeff told him. "Wasn't sure what I might need. Probably brought too much."

"I know how that is. Shouldn't be too long a wait." Remembering the flights when he had met Mitchell Robbins, Josh said, "Guess your flight was okay. Did you meet any interesting people?"

"No. I slept most of the time."

When they exited the terminal, Josh picked up one of Jeff's suitcases and told them, "I'll get the truck and pick you up here."

Jerilyn was remembering when she came for Austen's wedding and Josh met her at the airport. They hardly knew each other, but each had dreams of being together sometime. There was no kiss then, and none during the time she was there, even though she was staying in his extra room. And still no kiss when he took her to the airport for her trip home.

Somehow, despite those feelings for each other, and initial communication by phone, text, and email, their separation of so many miles and not being together led to each believing the other had established a relationship with someone else. Thank goodness they learned differently. There was finally a first kiss and a wedding.

Josh noticed the thoughtful look on his wife's face and wondered what it meant, even asking, "Everything okay?"

"Absolutely. I was just remembering when you picked me up here when I came for Austen's and Mark's wedding, and thinking about how much has changed and how happy I am to be with you for always."

Josh kissed her and said, "Me, too."

~

On the way to their house, they told him that though Martie had extra duties as Mother of the Bride, she had invited them all for a meal that evening. He had looked forward to seeing and being with Martie again, but his dream about Joyce had lingered in his memory. What might that mean? And how would he feel when he saw her?

Jeff was glad to have the extra time. When they got to Josh's and Jerilyn's house, they took him to the room that would be his for these few days. Jerilyn noticed a bemused look on her father's face, wondering what it might mean, then told him, "I hope you'll be comfortable. This is the room I used when I visited."

"I'm sure I will be. Was trying to remember the last time I might have slept in a bed other than the one at home. Maybe some time when we were on vacation."

They showed him through the rest of the house, ending in the kitchen. "It's going to be awhile before we go to Mattie's. Thought you might be hungry, maybe need a snack."

"Well, yes, I am," Jeff told his daughter. "But I don't want to spoil my appetite."

Jerilyn had made a favorite pizza snack, something Jeff had always liked but hadn't made it for years.

"This is perfect," he told her.

He called Jon instead of texting to let him know he was in Plattsford. "I'm at Jerilyn's and Josh's; had a snack even though we're going to Martie's for a meal. But breakfast was early, and I was hungry. Probably a good thing I slept on the plane, otherwise might need a nap.

"Any more plans for your wedding?"

Jon told him, "I have talked to Pastor Bradley and Jack is going to be my best man."

"Good. Well, I need to clean up a bit and change clothes for the trip to Martie's. Take care, bye."

"To you, too, Dad."

Jeff opened his suitcase and checked through the clothes he had brought, wondering what to wear when they went to Martie's. He remembered how much time it took when he was home to select what to pack. Now, he wondered why he chose the ones he did.

While he was changing clothes, he was remembering when Martie was in his home, that week before Christmas after Jack's wedding. *What did I wear then? Sure don't think I spent any time considering what it might be.* Most of his wardrobe was jeans and casual shirts and had been for some years.

Nineteen

On the drive to Martie's house, the dream about Joyce returned to Jeff's mind. He closed his eyes, trying to focus on details. It had been so real. As her image faded away, there was an expression on her face that seemed to be a sweet goodbye. Was she giving him permission to love again?

~

Waiting at home for Josh, Jerilyn, and Jefferson to arrive, Martie was nervous, questioning why she had planned this meal. It really was an unneeded extra for this week. But she did know why—Jefferson Tate.

They were in touch often, by email, text, phone, and even occasionally a letter. Martie was glad for each of those means of communication, especially the calls when she could hear Jefferson's voice. Still unexpected, she had never thought after losing Andrew, the love of her life, that another would create an extra heartbeat, a longing to love again.

She and Jefferson had experienced so few together times, but she had treasured them all. They had danced at wedding receptions, an opportunity to be in his arms, and there had been hugs. Martie remembered the last one when she, Josh, and Jerilyn left Jefferson's home after Christmas. She had wanted to kiss him and felt he wanted to kiss her, but it hadn't happened. Would it ever?

~

Before they got to Mattie's, Jeff asked, "Are Nancy and Mitchell going to join us tonight?"

Jerilyn told him, "No. She'll drive in tomorrow for the rehearsal. Her dress is at Mattie's, and she'll spend the night with her and get ready for the wedding there. Not sure about Mitchell.

"Do you know?" she asked her husband.

"I don't know either, but don't expect he will be at Mom's tonight."

Jerilyn laughed and agreed, "Probably not."

She and Josh were remembering that day in December when they left her dad's house and the way both he and Mattie had seemed so sad. They couldn't help wondering what their reaction would be when they were face-to-face in just a few more minutes.

~

Martie had been watching for them, so was standing at the open door as soon as they stopped in the driveway. Jefferson smiled and waved as he stepped out of the pickup and headed to where she waited.

Josh and Jerilyn were walking slowly behind Jeff. They had noted the happy smiles on their parents' faces and almost felt like intruders.

Martie and Jefferson were focused on each other. She had opened the door and walked toward him as he moved toward her. When they reached each other, their hands clasped as they smiled, looking into the other's face, then their arms pulled them into a hug.

Still holding each other, they leaned back, smiling again, then a closer hug and a kiss, tentative at first.

Josh and Jerilyn had expected the hug. It was obvious the older couple was always happy to be together, but they were not prepared for the kiss. They had stayed back, giving their parents space. Now they looked at each other with questions on their mind. Had Jeff and Martie kissed at one of the previous times they had been together?

At the end of the kiss, Martie and Jefferson stood for a while, heads resting against each other. It was as much a surprise to them as to their children. And what about their children? There was no way they could have missed it. Jeff wondered what they may have thought about it.

By the time Josh and Jerilyn returned their attention to the older couple, they were standing apart, facing them. Martie said, "Come on, it's time to eat."

~

The table was set and Martie asked them to take a seat. It was a simple meal—meatloaf, mashed potatoes and gravy, broccoli, a salad, and hot rolls. The bowls and dishes were on the table, and each one served themselves after Martie gave thanks. "Thank you, Father, for this time we can be together and for this food. Bless it to our bodies. Amen."

Josh said, "Mom, it's been awhile since you made this meatloaf. I had forgotten how good it is."

Jerilyn and her dad both agreed with Jeff admitting, "I've never had meatloaf made this way, with cheese and the meat rolled together like a jelly roll."

"I need to get the recipe," Jerilyn said. "Learn how to make it. Seems like it might be a favorite.

"Do you think you might want to make it sometime, Dad?"

"No."

At the surprised look on his daughter's face, he continued. "I'm pretty much living alone now and will be after Jon's wedding. I'll look forward to having it with you or Martie," glancing at her as he said her name.

Since their kiss, unexpected even to them, it was as if they didn't know how to act.

Now Martie smiled, then told them all, "There's cherry pie if anyone wants dessert."

Jefferson said, "This wonderful meal, plus pie. You must have been in the kitchen all day."

"I didn't make the pie," Martie admitted. "Got it from Eddie's."

They all decided they would like a small slice, and Josh had made a fresh pot of coffee for those who might want a cup.

~

After their meal, they worked together to get the kitchen cleaned. Then, taking a second cup of coffee, they moved to the living room.

It was obvious to Josh and Jerilyn that though their parents' kiss had seemed to surprise them, they did want to spend more time together, not wait for the busyness of the next day.

Josh turned to Jerilyn and said, "Oh, Honey, I forgot to get aspirin."

"I need paper towels too," Jerilyn told him.

"Guess we can go by the store on the way home. Mom, do you need anything?"

Martie told him, "I do need coffee, but you would have to come back by here. Tomorrow is going to be busy enough without unnecessary errands."

"We could leave Dad here so you can visit a bit longer, pick him up when we bring your coffee," Jerilyn said.

Josh had been watching their parents and could tell they were pleased with that idea. They both smiled and said, "That sounds good."

When their children left, Jefferson and Martie were glad to have the time together, but there was still a feeling of tension. Finally, there were smiles and, hand in hand, they went to the sofa so they could sit together.

Martie asked, "What do you think about that trip to the store?"

"I think it was made up—to give us a few minutes with just us."

"Me too," Martie agreed.

"But I'm glad."

Again, Martie said, "Me too,"

Squeezing his hand, she said, "I'm so glad you came for the wedding."

"I wouldn't have missed it. Might as well admit it was mainly because I wanted to see you. Though I could visit Jerilyn anytime and maybe see you too."

"It would be good if we lived closer together," Martie said. "Wouldn't require such a production, waiting for someone to get married."

"There are Jon and Linda getting married in June. Can't think of anyone else."

"Well, there is Mitchell's cousin," Martie told him. "He's in OP and I think he and his girlfriend are getting serious. Remember? She's Jayden's sister."

"Ah. If I had known that, it had slipped out of my mind.

"Enough speculation about weddings; the kids will be back soon. And, if it's okay with you, I'd like another kiss."

Martie smiled and said, "It's okay."

They turned so they were facing each other. His arms went around her, pulling her close, hers wrapped around him. They smiled, then moved into a kiss, tentative at first but changing into one filled with feeling and yearning and surprise.

When the kiss ended, they kept their arms around each other, drawing their heads back, looking into the other's eyes, then moved into another kiss, one that seemed more meaningful.

They knew Josh and Jerilyn would be back soon, and though they had witnessed that kiss when they first arrived, Jefferson and Martie wanted to keep this time to themselves. They separated but stayed on the sofa.

Jeff told her, "I never expected to have this kind of feeling again, so strong that I wanted to be with someone."

"Nor I," Martie echoed.

Those sober thoughts were on their minds and reflected on their faces when Josh and Jerilyn returned. Seeing that made them think the outcome of their parents' time together was different than they expected.

Josh held the bag with his mother's coffee and handed it to her.

"Oh, thank you so much! What flavor did you get?"

With a look of surprise, Josh asked, "Was there a certain flavor you wanted?"

Laughing, Martie said, "No. But you didn't ask. There could have been."

She turned away, smiling at the puzzled look on her son's face.

The coffee was still in her hand as she followed them all to the door. There were "goodbyes," and "see you tomorrow," from them all.

Jeff had hung back, letting Josh and Jerilyn go ahead of him. He took Martie's hand and told her, "Thanks again for the supper," then hugged her.

She stayed at the door, then waved as they backed out of the driveway and headed toward Josh's and Jerilyn's home. She took the coffee to the kitchen, then headed for her bedroom, a sweet smile on her face, remembering the hugs and kisses and how they made her feel.

In the pickup with Jerilyn and Josh, Jefferson was feeling the same, happy that there had finally been a kiss. Josh caught a glimpse of him in the rearview mirror. Jeff's eyes were closed, but there was a satisfied smile.

Twenty

artie was in bed, and before sleep overtook her, there were still thoughts of Jefferson on her mind. Would anything ever come of those special feelings? Could anything ever come of them? They lived so far apart, they were both settled in their homes and communities. They weren't old, but not young either, not as easy to make major changes in their life like Josh and Jerilyn did.

Was there a reason that her meeting with Jefferson produced such a strong emotion? One she hadn't felt since Andrew. As she drifted off to sleep, she thought, *I'm sure Jefferson feels the same.*

Martie stayed in bed for a while after waking, trying to remember details of the dream she barely recalled.

She had snuggled against Andrew, he turned and wrapped her in his arms. *"I love you so much,"* she told him. They moved to get closer together. He kissed her, smiled, then slowly faded away.

Martie hadn't dreamed about Andrew for such a long time. When she thought about his smile, she wondered if there was a meaning to it. Are there ever meanings to dreams? She knew that though it was going to be a busy day—filled with so much joy and happiness, the dream would stay in her thoughts.

Father,

I thank you for the dream—so unexpected, but so real—to be with Andrew on this special day. Is there a message for me? Was there meaning in the smile? You know my feelings for Jefferson Tate. Did the smile represent permission for me to love again? Thank you for all the blessings I receive.

In Jesus' name,

Amen.

Now, Martie, get yourself up. There's much to do—it's the day of Nancy's wedding rehearsal.

As she did every morning, Martie opened a devotional book to the day's date with its special words and Bible verses. After giving thanks for her breakfast, she ate while she read the words.

The verses were from Proverbs thirty, verses eighteen and nineteen. In her Bible, the chapter was headed *Wise Words from Agur.* In verse eighteen, he wrote, *There are three things that are too hard for me, really four I don't understand.* He listed them in verse nineteen, the fourth was, *and the way a man and woman fall in love.*

Martie thought, *If this wise man who wrote part of Proverbs doesn't understand, how can we humble, ordinary humans do so? Perhaps the best thing is to accept the love as a gift from God and do all we can to deserve it.*

～

Jeff was awake before Jerilyn and Josh. It was usual for him to get up early when he was home and that would be an hour earlier than Plattsford, Nebraska. He was hungry but didn't want to disturb his hosts stumbling around trying to find something to eat.

I'll stay in bed and think about Martie. This will be a busy day for her.

Hope she's not too tired from yesterday. I wonder if she might be thinking of me even though she has enough other things, important things, to think about.

He closed his eyes, remembering the kisses. *Might there be others? I'll be here a few more days. Maybe there'll be a chance for us to be alone, go someplace together. A time to get better acquainted, learn more about each other.*

Jeff wasn't sure how that could happen. He had no vehicle, though he could probably borrow Jerilyn's or Josh's. Maybe Martie could provide the transportation. He smiled thinking about that. He could picture Martie parking in the driveway, walking to the door and knocking. Josh or Jerilyn would answer, and she would ask, "Is Jefferson here?"

He fell back asleep, the smile still on his face, then woke to a knock on the door and his daughter asking, "Dad, are you awake?"

"Ah, yes, I am. Was awake earlier, surprised I went back to sleep."

Josh was making a big breakfast. It was going to be a busy day. Not sure if there would be time for lunch and it would be awhile before the rehearsal dinner.

~

Jerilyn and Josh were both part of the wedding party, so when they got to the church, Jeff felt like a fifth wheel. He did have opportunity to get acquainted with Mitch's family and learn about their ranch.

Dennis told him, "If you're going to be here for a while, maybe you can visit us."

"Sounds good," Jeff said. "Never been to a ranch. But I'm dependent on somebody else to provide transportation for me."

"If not now, maybe another time," Dennis said. "Since your daughter lives here."

~

Rehearsal dinner was at TrailWays in their new building that had been built for year-round events. Having heard much about TW, Jeff was glad to experience its ambience. Everyone liked the building and expected it would be a popular venue in the future.

Jeff and Martie were sitting together, and their children noticed how they were enjoying the circumstance.

As she watched, Nancy said, "I wonder if they have kissed."

Josh and Jerilyn both said, "Yes, we even saw it."

She wasn't surprised, but that affirmation seemed to trouble her, though she had no good reason to feel that way. Nancy liked Jeff, who was now her brother's father-in-law. Perhaps it was because she was getting married and she was sad that her father could be no part of it.

She would be spending the night with her mother, where she would get ready for her wedding the next day. *I wonder if she will say anything about her time with Jefferson. It is good to see her happiness. It's like there's a glow around her.*

All the Robbins family would be driving back to their ranches, about a fifty-mile drive. They would bring their clothes for the wedding when they drove in the next day and would change clothes at the church.

~

Family and friends filled the church for the wedding. Lennie and Billy, the young men who were hands at the Rocking R, were excited to be ushers, dressed in tuxedos. Jefferson was seated on the bride's side, next to where Martie would sit after giving her daughter away.

When the music started, the pastor, groom, and male attendants, Josh, Mitchell's cousin Nate, and his brother-in-law Ronnie, entered and walked to the raised area in front. Then came Mitchell's sister Sandy, his cousin Judy, and matron of honor Jerilyn, as well as ring bearer David and flower girl Emma.

When the music changed to "Here Comes the Bride," Nancy entered, escorted by her mother. When asked, "Who gives this woman to this man?" Martie said, "I do." She went with her daughter to Mitchell, placed Nancy's hand in his, and told him, "Love her and take care of her."

Pastor Sanders welcomed all and told them how the couple had met, turned to them, and cautioned them to always love each other. There were the vows, exchange of rings, and the pastor saying, "You may kiss your bride."

"Ladies and gentlemen, Mr. and Mrs. Mitchell Robbins."

Jeff, noticing tears in Martie's eyes, took her hand and squeezed it, giving her a smile. He mouthed, "Okay?" She nodded and returned the squeeze.

When it was time for the recessional, Jefferson walked with Martie. She had taken his arm as they moved to the aisle. The move surprised him, pleasing him at the same time. He looked down at her with a smile as she looked into his face with one of her own.

Wanting to have her dad as part of the wedding, Nancy and her mother had discussed the best way to do so. They chose a picture of Andrew Wilson with his daughter to display at the reception.

Jeff studied the picture thinking, *he is a handsome man*, but was unable to picture him with Martie. At the same time, he was remembering his wife, Joyce, and how he missed her. *I'd so love to still have you with me.*

Looking around for Martie, he saw that she was holding Mitchell's baby niece. When he reached her, she asked, "Isn't she sweet?" They had both mentioned at different times how they would like to have grandchildren. Now both of Martie's children, and two of his, were married. Did any of them plan to have kids?

All the young people were dancing, including the cowboy ushers, with some girls about the same age as they. Jeff answered Martie's question with, "Yes, she is. But why don't you give her back to her grandmother? I'd like to dance if you agree."

They had hardly begun to dance when Josh and Jerilyn came to them. They had also beckoned for Nancy and Mitchell to join them. Jerilyn told the group, "We have some news. I'm pregnant."

There were hugs and smiles and, of course, the question, "When?" "October."

Jefferson and Martie smiled at each other and, with excitement, hugged their kids and said, "We're going to be grandparents!"

Some people who were close enough to hear were puzzled, having no idea of what their relationship was. Those who did know decided if it mattered, they would learn.

Twenty-One

The families were still reflecting on the baby news when Mitchell's cousin—Nate Williams, his best man—let them know, "According to the schedule, it's time for the bouquet toss."

There was quite a group when the unmarried ladies gathered, including the dance partners of the cowboy ushers, as well as Emma, the four-year-old flower girl. She assured her mom it was okay for her to be there as, "I'm not married."

Nate's girlfriend, Carly Black, caught it. The young ushers were relieved, and Emma cried. Carly's sister Jayden's bouquet had landed on the floor between her and Linda. All who had witnessed that wondered if there was any tradition about such an occurrence.

~

Sparklers were passed out to the wedding guests as they went outside to send off the newlyweds. They lined up, facing each other, to form a pathway and the sparklers were lit. They waved them around as Nancy and Mitchell, hand in hand, made their way to his convertible, then waved at everyone as they began their journey.

It could be considered usual for there to be an anticlimactic aura after the just-married couple left, a sort of sadness mixed with the joy. And Jefferson and Martie had a new, unexpected joy. She also knew she was going to feel lonely at home after having Nancy there for a few days, along with the excitement of the wedding.

Jerilyn noticed the different emotions passing over her mother-in-law's face and guessed at the reason.

"Martie, would it be all right if we come to your place before heading on home?"

"Oh, that would be wonderful! We can talk more about the baby." Turning to Jerilyn's father, she asked, "Jefferson, why don't you ride with me?"

No one could miss his smile when he said, "I'll be glad to."

~

As they were walking to his pickup, Josh asked Jerilyn, "So why are we going to Mom's?"

"I was watching her. She's glad for the marriage and the baby, but sad to go home, be by herself."

"How did you come to that conclusion, just watching her face?" Josh asked.

"I'm a woman," Jerilyn answered.

"Guess that's as good a reason as any," her husband admitted.

Jerilyn told him, "Even you couldn't have missed the excitement and joy knowing she wouldn't have to be alone."

"And having Jeff at her house again," Josh said. "And riding with her in her car."

Jerilyn said, "Yeah. How do you feel about that?"

"How do you feel?"

"I have to admit, it's not something I ever thought might happen," Jerilyn said. "Dad has always been … well, Dad. I know he and Mom loved each other so much; they were like one entity. And no question he has missed her. Also no question Dad likes your mom very much—maybe even loves her."

"Yeah."

~

They had reached Martie's house. She and Jefferson had pulled into the driveway ahead of their children but were still in the car. So the four walked to the house together.

When they were inside, they looked around at each other, all still in the fancy, dressy clothes they had worn for the wedding. Jeff's were the least formal since he had been only a guest.

Now he said, "You know, you all probably ended up in some of the pictures that were taken. I wasn't, as far as I know, but would like to be in one with all of you. Any of you good with selfies?"

They decided that they would each take one to assure there would be at least one good one, so they spent several minutes doing so.

After all the merriment—the laughing and the posing, Martie said, "Probably none of you is hungry, but I do have some lemon bars, and I could make coffee or …"

That appealed to all of them, so they went to the kitchen and took chairs around the table. With the refreshments in front of them, Martie took the hands of Jefferson and Josh, then with all holding hands, she said, "Let's give thanks. Father, we thank you for this special day—the joining of our family with another, and for the expected baby. We pray your blessings on all of us and for this repast. In Jesus' name, amen."

There was much conversation while they enjoyed the dessert and coffee. Jeff and Martie learned that their children were going to wait until its birth to learn the gender of their baby. "So we'll be considering names for both boys and girls. Do you have any suggestions you'd like for us to ponder?"

~

It had been a long day for all of them, and Jerilyn, especially, was tired. "I need to get out of this dress and into something more comfortable, like pajamas."

She and Josh hugged his mom and told her, "See you at church tomorrow," then headed to their pickup, leaving Jeff and Martie to have a few more minutes alone.

They had been together enough that each recognized their growing feelings for the other. But there was still a certain nervousness when it was just the two of them.

Jefferson told Martie, "I've enjoyed today—being with you. Guess I'll see you tomorrow at church?"

"Yes," Martie assured him. "Have been thinking that I've been with you at your church. It will be good to have you there."

They had moved together as they headed toward the door, and Jeff took her hands. There were smiles, then their arms went around each other, and there was a kiss, more smiles, then a deeper one.

He told Martie, "Guess I better get to the pickup; kids are probably wondering. Sleep well, see you tomorrow. Bye."

"You, too."

They were still hand in hand at the door, then another quick kiss and a wave.

≈

At breakfast Sunday morning, Jerilyn asked Jeff, "Dad, did we tell you we have to be back in our classrooms tomorrow and the rest of the week?"

"Sorry. If you did, I don't remember."

"Martie knows," she told him. "And I think she may have some ideas to occupy your time." His daughter noted the happy, expectant look on Jeff's face when he heard that.

"Also, Mark Thomas told us he would be glad to provide transportation to the airport for your flight home.

"I hope you don't feel we are abandoning you. Maybe you can spend a morning or afternoon at school with us." There was a nod from him. "We need to plan something special for Tuesday evening.

"And if I haven't told you or let you know, I'm so glad you're here." With those words, she gave him a hug.

≈

When Josh and Jerilyn and her father entered church, Martie was waiting for them. They headed toward the area where the Wilsons usually sat. Several people who had been at the wedding the day before told Jeff they were glad to see him again. They asked, "Are you going to be in Plattsford for a while?"

He told them, "I'll be here a few more days, then it's back home."

"Where is home?"

"Overland Park, Kansas. It's a suburb of Kansas City."

They reached the row where the Thomas family was already seated and scooted in next to them. Jefferson made sure to sit beside

Martie. Those two didn't notice, but Josh and Jerilyn didn't miss the surreptitious glances from some in the congregation.

At the end of service, some who hadn't greeted them earlier came to do so. Jeff speculated later that it could be out of curiosity. *Who is that man with Mattie?*

Mark Thomas waited so he could speak to Jeff. "Did Jerilyn tell you I'll be glad to take you to the airport?"

"Yes, she did. That's great."

"You can call or text me later about the time," Mark told him. "Josh and Jerilyn both have my number."

Talking among themselves while walking to their cars, the Wilsons and Jeff discussed lunch plans.

Martie said, "The kids know I often have Sunday lunch at Eddie's Café. How about us all going there?"

She had taken Jeff's arm, almost automatically. There was a silent communication between Josh and Jerilyn, who nodded that was a good idea.

With that, Martie said, "Okay. Why don't you ride with me?" to Jefferson, already leading him to her car. Their children couldn't help smiling as they climbed into their pickup.

~

While they were enjoying their meal, there was conversation about what Jefferson might do Monday and Tuesday to occupy his time. He reminded Jerilyn that she had mentioned having him visit school.

"Maybe I'll do that Tuesday. We can talk more about details tomorrow."

Josh and Jerilyn glanced at each other with a silent question, then nodded. Maybe they could plan something special, a bit different than a regular school day.

Then Jeff turned to Martie and said, "You mentioned having an idea for something to do Monday."

She flashed a perverse look toward her son, then said, "I know Dennis invited you to visit the ranch. Maybe we could do that. I would check with them first in case they might be busy with something.

"We could have lunch at Runza's in Scottsbluff, then to the Rocking R from there. And if it's not convenient to go to the ranch, we could just tour the city."

Jerilyn was watching her dad as Martie voiced her idea. She could see he would be happy to spend the day with Martie, whatever they ended up doing.

Twenty-Two

Martie and Jefferson would have liked to spend more of the day together, but both admitted they needed a nap.

"And you need to spend more time with your daughter," Martie told him. "I'll check with the Robbins and let you know about tomorrow."

Jeff walked with her to her car, and they were able to have a quick hug and kiss. He waited until she was driving away to go to the pickup parked nearby. He told his daughter and son-in-law that he did, indeed, need a nap.

Before going to his room, he asked them not to let him sleep long, looked at Jerilyn, and said, "Martie was right. I do need to spend time with you."

~

While Jeff slept, Josh and Jerilyn sat at the table with cups of coffee and slices of the pecan pie they had brought from Eddie's.

Josh said, "Sure is interesting, watching our parents."

"Yes. We need to talk about what we might do with Dad at school."

"I don't have any ideas," Josh told her. "Do you?"

"Yes, I do. Since he will be there Tuesday, we can tell our classes tomorrow that there will be a special guest the next day—either morning or afternoon, depending on which of our classes he visits first.

"We can interview him, then ask him to tell the class about his police career, maybe his life in general? Then ask if they have any questions."

Watching Josh, she asked, "You don't think that's a good idea?"

"Well, not bad. But do you think that will take up two hours of time?"

"Maybe," Jerilyn admitted. "Guess it depends how curious the kids are. Do you have a better thought?"

Laughing, Josh said, "No."

"We need to ask Dad anyway. He might think of something better."

"Better than what?" Jeff had just entered the room and heard his daughter's statement.

Jerilyn told him they were discussing what they might do on Tuesday when he would be at school with them.

"So, what are we doing?"

"Not sure." Then she told him what their ideas were.

Jeff said, "That sounds okay. Probably as good as anything. We'll just have to wait and see, play it by ear. Maybe I could ask them questions about their lives.

"Now, looks like we're having pie?"

"Yes," his daughter said. "Want some coffee with it?"

"Sure."

Josh and Jerilyn joined him at the table, having a second cup. Then she said, "We haven't had a chance to just visit since you've been here. Anything extraordinary happening in Overland Park?"

~

Martie had a nap also. When she woke up, she went to the kitchen and made coffee. As she enjoyed a cup, along with a slice of the coconut cream pie she had brought from Eddie's, her mind turned to earlier in the day.

She especially thought of church with Jefferson beside her. Some people had been at the wedding the day before, so weren't completely surprised. Had any of them overheard their declaration? "We're going to be grandparents!"

Now she smiled as she remembered the bewilderment exhibited on the face of others. Some of them were also at Eddie's. Yes, she was sure there would be questions. What might her answer be? She hadn't considered that before. Did Jefferson get questions after people saw them together at his church? If so, what were his answers?

Wanting to dismiss those thoughts for now, she recalled how she felt having him sitting beside her. Could she even describe it? She had not expected to ever again have opportunity to sit beside a special man. Yes, Jefferson was special to her, and she believed she was special to him. Still, what could ever come of it beyond a mostly long-distance affair? Could one even consider it being an affair if they didn't see each other?

Well, we're going to spend Monday together. I need to call Dennis Robbins to determine whether it will be convenient for us to visit the ranch. If not, what might we do instead?

Martie learned when she called Dennis that it wasn't going to be a good time for her and Jefferson to visit. Some rodeo representative would be there to examine and possibly buy some calves.

Dennis suggested, "Maybe you can make a trip to visit us next time Jeff is visiting."

She waited until Monday morning to call Jefferson. When he answered, she said, "I'm sorry, can't visit the ranch today," and told him why.

He asked, "Can we still spend the day together?"

"Absolutely," she assured him. "I have some ideas. Have you had breakfast? Thought I could pick you up and we can decide together what to do."

"Just finished breakfast. I'll clear the table, brush my teeth, and be ready when you get here. Goodbye."

"And to you."

What might the day be like? It doesn't matter to me what we might do. I'll have the whole day with Martie.

Jefferson smiled. He was still surprised at how happy he felt, especially with that extra beat of his heart just from talking on the phone with her. He intended to enjoy this day and try not to be concerned about after.

He and Martie would still be in different states, hours and hundreds of miles apart. If they were to eventually be together, it would happen in God's time, and they would trust in Him as they worked out where that would be. Jefferson had his home in Overland Park, Kansas, the city he had lived in all his life.

And Martie had one here, in Plattsford, Nebraska. She hadn't lived in town all her life, but always in its environs in the country. But maybe he was assuming too much. Maybe what there is now is all there will ever be.

Martie drove up with that last thought, got out of the car, and hurried to the door. She was ready to start the day with Jefferson. He had been watching for her and opened the door before she had a chance to knock. They stood smiling at each other, then a quick hug.

He had the key in his hand and locked the door. Martie was holding her car key and asked, "Would you like to drive?"

"No," he told her. "You know where we're going, and I will enjoy having you chauffeuring me. So where are we going?"

She said, "I know you haven't visited this part of the country, so everything will be new. I was thinking, though, since we aren't visiting the Robbins Ranch, we might drive to the ranch that we owned. I haven't been there for quite some time.

"You might get an idea about how our life changed. I didn't know until recently how much it affected Nancy. She's so happy she will be living on a ranch again."

Jefferson let her continue talking about what they might do, enjoying the sound of her voice as he sat beside her.

Martie continued, "And, of course, you'll see some of our Nebraska countryside."

Now he said, "That all sounds good to me. Though one doesn't need to drive very many miles from our house in Overland Park to be in the country, that hasn't happened recently. Maybe that's something I'll do when I'm home. Sure isn't anything keeping me in the house.

"Jayden's family has some acreage. In fact, Mitch's cousin Nate boards his horse there." Jefferson seemed to be thinking out loud as he considered the possibility of exploring, sightseeing, visiting in the country. "Maybe I'll drive to their place, see what it's like."

~

Martie and Jefferson didn't know what to expect, but it was a most wonderful day for them. There had been times in the past when Martie visited the Butlers, the people who had bought the ranch. They had been friends and told her they would be glad to see her any time.

Seeing her with Jefferson piqued their curiosity, which was enhanced when they learned how they had met. The Butlers could see the two had special feelings for each other.

Jeff had never visited a ranch, so when the Butlers offered to give them a tour, he was ready. Martie was curious to see what might have changed in the past few years.

Ted Butler asked, "Would you like to ride or take the pickup?"

"I've never had opportunity to ride," Jeff told them. "Maybe someday. So I vote for the pickup."

Though it had been normal those years ago for Martie to ride, she said, "Maybe another time."

They enjoyed checking out different aspects of the ranch, learning what the main activity was and getting acquainted or reacquainted. At the end of the tour, they were invited to have a simple lunch with the Butlers.

Martie thanked them, but told them, "I kind of planned to take Jefferson to a restaurant in Plattsford," glancing at him for his reaction, which was to nod his head, "yes."

They were in Martie's car, headed back to Plattsford when she asked Jefferson what he had thought of the ranch.

"Educational. Hadn't thought of all the different aspects, what's required for a successful, working ranch," he said. "Are there any changes from when you lived there?"

She told him, "We didn't have the big game hunting, but it seems to be popular."

"How long did you live there?"

"A bit more than eighteen years."

Jefferson could tell there was a sadness surrounding her memories, so he stayed silent.

Then Martie said, "Thought I would take another route back to town, drive by where my folks' farm was, let you see a bit more of our country."

"Okay."

"Then we'll go to The Place, a restaurant in Plattsford, for lunch, then home."

~

Lunch for them was later than it usually would have been, and after the tour of the ranch and the drive through the country, both were tired, feeling like they needed a nap. Kind of an awkward situation.

Martie finally said, "I'm tired, looks like you are too. But I want to spend more time with you, visit more, not take you back to Josh's yet. How about you take off your shoes, rest on the couch? I'll go to my room for my nap. I'll set the time on my phone, so it won't be too long— thirty minutes?"

They had walked hand in hand from the car to the house. But when it was decided they would take naps, Jefferson walked her to the door of her room and said, "I'd like a hug if it's okay with you."

Martie smiled and said, "Absolutely. And I want a kiss."

Jefferson pulled her into his arms, and hers went around him. They smiled, hugged, then came the kiss, the one they had both looked forward to since the day began. They drew their heads back, searched the other's face, then another smile, and another kiss. Then with no words, they each went to the place where they might nap for a while.

Martie would have liked to leave the door to her bedroom open but closed it, set the time on her phone, removed her shoes, and climbed onto her bed. She closed her eyes and prayed. *Father, you know the feelings I have for Jefferson. I think he may feel the same toward me. I don't know if there will ever be more than these brief times together. Whatever it is to be, I pray I can accept and be content.*

Twenty-Three

Josh and Jerilyn arrived home after school. They had told their students there would be a special guest the next day but gave no hint as to who it would be. The kids had all seemed excited. Perhaps it was only because it would be a change from the regular school day.

They decided to have Jeff go to Josh's class in the morning. Now, Jerilyn asked, "So, how are you going to introduce Dad?"

"Oh, guess I need to think about that. Any ideas?"

His wife told him, "You're pretty smart, you should be able to come up with something."

At her words, he moved toward her, a mischievous look on his face. "Oh, you think I'm smart, do you?"

As he started toward her, she made to move away, but he reached her, wrapped his arms around her, and said, "I think you're smart too," then kissed her smiling lips.

"And I love you so much. Not sure I've told you that today."

"I love you too," Jerilyn assured him and kissed him back.

"Wonder what our parents did today, and when your mom will bring my dad home."

Josh asked, "Should we call, see if everything's okay?"

"I am curious. But they're our parents, not our kids."

"Maybe this is a rehearsal for when we have kids."

Jerilyn made no response, just gave him a humorous look.

~

Jefferson and Martie had actually considered that their kids might be wondering about the day and when he would be back to their house. So, just as Josh and Jerilyn were talking about getting in touch with their parents, her dad called.

"Dad, we were just talking about you."

"All good, I hope."

"Of course. So how has your day been?"

Jefferson gave a brief report about where they had gone, what they had done. "We had a late lunch, but if you haven't had supper yet, thought we might bring a pizza to share with you?"

"Sounds good, but if you haven't already picked one up, why don't I call to have one delivered? What kind would you like?"

Jeff and Martie chose to let Josh and Jerilyn choose the pizza and whatever else to go with it. They were glad to have more time together after their naps.

They learned more about each other, including what their lives had been like growing up. As expected, they were very different— the city guy and country girl. They had fun comparing and wondering what their relationship might have been like if they had lived in the same area when they were growing up, maybe attending the same school.

There was no conclusion to those thoughts. What had actually occurred in their lives clouded any imaginings.

Jefferson said, "It doesn't matter anyway. God led us to meet at this time in our lives, and I'm glad." He smiled, took Martie's hand, and kissed it.

She agreed, "Me, too," releasing her hand so she could give him a hug.

They were in Martie's car heading toward Josh and Jerilyn's home when she said, "This may be the last time we'll be together before you go home."

Jefferson felt a punch in his stomach at her words. Seemed like he had just arrived. But she was right, he would be at school with Jerilyn and Josh on Tuesday then leave Wednesday morning.

When they arrived, thinking again about Martie's recent words, they stayed in the car, each staring through the windshield, yet so completely aware of the other.

Jefferson took Martie's hands, and they turned toward each other. He told her again how much he had enjoyed the day, then asked, "What will you be doing tomorrow?"

"Don't have any plans. Guess I'm wondering if there might be a possibility of us being together. Maybe after school? But no idea what it would be," Martie said. "You really haven't spent much time with your daughter. And that's important."

Jefferson nodded, then said, "Guess we need to go in, see if the pizza has been delivered and what else there might be."

Martie smiled and said, "Yes. They're probably wondering why we're still sitting out here."

Jefferson got out and went around the front where Martie was waiting for him. He took her hand, leaned down to give her a kiss, then led her to the house.

Josh answered the door as soon as they knocked and said, "Good to see you. Come in."

When they got to the kitchen, Jerilyn hugged both of them and asked, "Did you have a good day?"

Martie and Jefferson glanced at each other, smiled, and nodded, "Yes, we did."

Though Jeff had already given a short synopsis of the day, while they were eating, Josh wanted to know more about their trip to the ranch where he had grown up.

His mother said, "Don't know if you remember I used to visit occasionally a few years ago. Everything is pretty much the same, except for expected changes that occur through the passage of years. There is one change that surprised me, maybe not you."

"You've sure raised my curiosity," Josh said. "What is it?"

"Big game hunting."

Josh exhibited obvious surprise at her answer. "Boy, I must really be behind times. Would never have guessed that would be an activity at a ranch in Nebraska. How long have they been doing that?"

"Don't know. They didn't say," Martie told him.

"Well, maybe I need to make a visit when school's out."

Jerilyn added, "I'd like to see where you grew up too."

They all enjoyed the rest of the evening, and too soon, Martie said, "I've loved this. It's been a most wonderful day, but I want to get home before it gets any darker."

It was easy to see she was sad to be leaving, not sure when she would see Jefferson again.

Jerilyn hugged her and asked, "Will you be all right? Would you like for one of us to follow you home?"

Laughing, Martie told her, "I'll be all right. But I've been so happy to spend time with your dad, I haven't even asked how you are feeling and if my son is taking good care of you. Think you know how excited I am about the coming baby."

"Yes, no question," Jerilyn told her.

Martie hugged Jerilyn and her son, told them she'd let them know when she got home. Then Jefferson took her hand to walk her to her car. When he came back in, the younger couple noticed the tears in his eyes.

He told them, "Think I'll turn in—a busy day tomorrow."

Twenty-Four

Tuesday morning was a bit hectic with three adults preparing for the day. They all drove to school together in Josh's pickup. On the way, Jefferson said, "Can't remember last time I was in an elementary school."

Looking out the windows, he noticed several children walking, and wondered if any of them might be in either Jerilyn's or Josh's class. After they had parked and were all heading toward the school, some of the students seemed to have been waiting for them. Perhaps to see who the special guest was.

There was a chair set aside for Jeff in the classroom. Josh stood at the open door, welcoming the fifteen students as they entered. They each glanced toward Jeff before taking their seats.

There were the usual beginning exercises, then Josh said, "Yesterday I told you we would have a special guest today." He walked to Jeff and continued, "I want to introduce former Police Lieutenant Jefferson Lawrence Tate. He is also my father-in-law.

"He spent thirty years with the Overland Park, Kansas, Police Department. He is going to tell you about his work. If you want, you can take notes. Maybe think of some questions you'd like to ask."

Reaching his hand toward him as an invitation to begin, he said, "Jeff."

Unexpectedly, the kids stood to applaud, bringing a smile to him. Jeff stood for a while, enjoying the spontaneous act, then raised his hands and said, "Thank you so much. I appreciate it."

When the students were settled back in their seats, he began his narration.

"As your teacher told you, I was on the Police Force thirty years, beginning with the patrol division, as most newbies do, and most often on the midnight shift."

He continued relating highlights, positive experiences, some not so positive, and some scary, leading to when he was promoted to Watch Commander.

"I have been retired for a few years now, but sometimes get together with other retired police officers I worked with. Occasionally visit the station where I spent most of my career. The City has grown a lot over the years, and there's an added station now.

"I'll end this by letting you know that one of my sons is now a Police Officer. My father was also one, so Jack is the third generation of Tates in the OPPD. Now, are there any questions?"

Josh was as interested as the students to hear the answers and wished he had thought to record the presentation. Maybe Jerilyn could do that when her father talked to her class after lunch.

When Jeff asked about any questions, it seemed like nearly everyone had one. Arms went up, trying to get his attention.

"Were you ever shot? Did you ever shoot anyone? Were you ever in a high-speed chase? What does a Watch Commander do? How many officers in Overland Park? Are there any women? Did you arrest anyone? What for?"

By the time all the questions had been asked and answered, it was lunchtime. Josh had not imagined it would use so much time and wondered if his class would be settled down for the afternoon.

Josh, Jerilyn, and Jeff sat together at lunch. Seemed like all of the students from Josh's class made a point of coming by to say, "Hi."

Smiling, Jeff said, "Makes me feel like some celebrity."

Josh told him, "I was amazed how the kids reacted. You did a great job. I enjoyed it too. Wished I had been prepared to record it." Turning to Jerilyn, he said, "Thought maybe we could do that in your class this afternoon."

"Sounds good. Can you get it set up?"

"Yes, I will."

~

The presentation in Jerilyn's classroom was pretty much the same as in Josh's, except when they realized Jerilyn was Jeff's daughter, the girls, especially, had questions for her, like, "How was it having a policeman for a dad? Did you ever date a police officer?"

When she was asked about dating a policeman, after answering, "No, I didn't," she thought of her friend, Jayden, who had dated Jerilyn's brother, Jack. And now they were married. Jayden had hinted to her once that being the wife of a policeman was probably different than being a daughter of one. *I think I understand that now, especially since Jack was shot on duty before he and Jayden were married.*

On their way home after school, Jeff's presentation was the main topic of their conversation and continued even as they entered the house.

Jeff asked, "Wonder what Martie would have thought of it. She might have had questions too."

At that statement, Josh and Jerilyn glanced at each other. Jeff would be leaving the next morning. Mark Thomas would pick him up to take him to the airport for his flight back to Kansas. They both knew their parents would like a bit more time together.

Jerilyn gestured for her husband to follow her as she moved toward the kitchen.

"How about ordering four chicken dinners from Eddie's? We can have them delivered to your mom's, then drive there with Dad. Won't stay late, but they'll have that bit more time."

"Sounds good to me. Want me to call her, let her know?"

Jerilyn said, "Please," then kissed him and told him, "I love you so much."

After ordering their meals, Josh called his mother.

"Josh. Is something wrong?"

"No. Hoping you haven't eaten yet."

"I haven't," Martie told him. "Checked in the fridge to see if anything appeals to me."

"Good," her son said. "We ordered chicken dinners to be delivered to you. We'll come and join you."

"Jefferson too?"

"Yes, Mom. It's obvious you two hoped for more time together. This way, we can all visit, talk about family history or whatever. Just can't stay very late with tomorrow's schedule."

While they waited to go to Martie's, Josh also called Mark Thomas to check plans for the trip to the airport.

At Martie's, Jefferson said to her, "You know that Jon and Linda are engaged. He called Jerilyn to congratulate her on the baby and told her they have a date."

Martie perked up at that, wondering when it was, thinking at the same time, *There's no reason to think I will be invited.*

"So, when is it?"

"The last Saturday in June."

"That soon?"

"Yes," Jefferson answered. "Seems like when my kids decide to get married, they don't want to wait."

Josh took Jerilyn's hand and said, "Maybe not much waiting after the decision. There was more than enough before."

He kissed his wife, recalling those many months when they weren't together and not even communicating.

Jerilyn knew Martie wondered if she might be invited. And Jerilyn knew she would be but chose not to share that information yet.

Martie continued pondering the possibility. Even if she was invited and attended, though it would be another wedding when she would be with Jefferson, what would happen after that? Their kids would all be married—no more weddings in their families.

Jerilyn watched her dad and her mother-in-law. No question they cared for each other, and that caring was growing every time they met. What might come of it?

She remembered the separations between her and Josh after their first meeting. Though not really expecting it would ever be more than a crush. After all, they lived in different states, hundreds of miles apart. Then realizing their feelings were much more than just a passing infatuation, they determined to rearrange their lives so they could be together always.

Maybe their parents felt the same. Jerilyn almost ached watching them. They had both had happy, long-term marriages, perhaps never expecting to have such a strong regard for another again. And along with those feelings, she perceived there was also a sense of guilt. Though they might want more, hope for a permanent outcome, should they nurture it?

Once they got past the discussion about the wedding, the four enjoyed talking about their families. Though one family had grown up in the country and the other in the city, they learned that many of their experiences were the same.

Too soon for Jefferson and Martie, it was time for him, Jerilyn, and Josh to leave. The young couple hugged Martie, told her they would be in touch, and told Jefferson they would wait for him in the car.

Jefferson and Martie moved to each other as soon as the others exited. There was a hug, then a kiss and tears from Martie.

"What are we going to do about us?" she asked. "What can we do about us? I'm always so glad to see you and so sad when I leave or you leave."

And though neither had previously expressed their feelings, she told Jefferson, "I think I love you."

Jeff's heart jumped at those words, and he told her, "I feel the same. How can that be? We have hardly had any time together."

"It doesn't always take time," Martie said. "Maybe we're ready for this kind of change in our lives."

"I'm sure you'll get an invitation to the wedding," Jefferson told her. "You'll come, won't you?"

"Yes."

"Guess I better leave. Glad we had the time together this week."

"Me too."

They walked to the door, one more kiss and Jefferson told her, "I'll let you know when I get home." Then headed to the car.

Martie watched till he opened the door and waved. She waved back, then shut her door, and sobbing, headed to the couch.

Twenty-Five

Jerilyn and Josh had to leave before Jeff would be picked up for the trip to the airport. Her dad was so obviously sad, Jerilyn considered taking the morning off.

Instead, she hugged him and told him, "I love you, Dad. So glad you came. Text me when you're home, okay?"

Jeff returned the hug and said, "I love you too. It was such a wonderful visit all around. Kind of different, visiting my daughter in her house."

Josh hugged him too and told him, "You were a good guest, come again."

Before she followed her husband out the door, Jerilyn asked Jeff, "Are you going to be okay?"

"I will be."

~

Mark Thomas arrived shortly after Josh and Jerilyn had left. Jeff's luggage was at the door, but before going out, he checked back through the house to be sure all appliances were off and he hadn't left anything. After locking the door, he gave the key to Mark to return to Josh later.

There was no conversation between the two men other than, "Hi," and, "Good Morning," until they were on the highway heading to Scottsbluff.

Martie was much in Jefferson's thoughts, and Mark could tell there was something weighing on the older man's mind. He didn't know what, but even he had observed the interaction between Jeff and Mattie Wilson. *Could that be it? A sadness that he wouldn't be seeing her?*

Finally, to break the silence, he asked Jeff, "So how has your visit to Nebraska been?"

"Okay. Would have been good to stay awhile longer." Smiling, he added, "Probably long enough for Jerilyn and Josh."

"Might you come again?"

"Probably," Jeff answered. "My daughter lives here, and," under his breath, "Martie."

Directing a quick glance at his passenger, Mark thought, *I was right.*

"Did you get a chance to see anything besides what's in Plattsford?"

"Well, there was that bit of TrailWays after the rehearsal," Jeff said. "And Martie took me on a tour one day. We visited the ranch her family had owned and drove by the farm where she grew up."

Almost as an afterthought, he added, "And I spent yesterday at the school where Josh and Jerilyn teach."

"Fairview."

"What?"

"The name of the school," Mark told him.

"Oh, yeah. I remember seeing it on the building."

Mark said, "Austen told me that Linda and Jon have a wedding date."

"Yeah, last Saturday in June."

"Not very long," Mark said.

"No."

Knowing that Jeff and Martie first met at a wedding and had both been at others, Mark wondered if she would be attending.

~

When Martie woke up, she glanced at the clock. She didn't know what time Jefferson's flight was. On one hand, wishing she had been the one who took him to the airport but knowing the drive home alone would have been difficult. She would remember the times they had been together these past few days and before, and the words they had said to each other. Jefferson had told her she would get an invitation to Jon and Linda's wedding. *Will I go? How can I not? I almost long to see him, be with him.* Even with those feelings of uncertainty, she had told him she would.

Despite anything else, his daughter still lived here, and there would be a grandchild too. No doubt, there would be visits. The possibility of her and Jefferson having a life together was more complicated.

But, she admitted to herself, *I would be content, happy wherever we are—if I could be with him.* Then she said a prayer for a safe trip for Jefferson and the next time they might be together, then got up to start her day.

She needed to check on her flower beds; they had been neglected for a few weeks while she was helping prepare for her daughter's wedding, as well as the time spent with Jefferson.

When she checked later, she found the flower beds were not in bad shape, only a few weeds to be pulled, and a few plants needing to be watered, nothing taking much time. She had her clippers, so gathered a small bouquet to enjoy. As always, she had her phone with her in case there was a call. She didn't want to miss hearing from Jefferson.

Her mind returned to her spontaneous declaration, "I think I love you."

Oh, Jefferson, there's no question, I can hardly bear not seeing you, being with you. Never expected to have those kind of feelings again. And for a man who lives so far away in another state.

Martie remembered visiting with her son those many months ago when there were similar concerns between him and Jerilyn. No idea that there would come a time she would have the same kind of feelings. And certainly not for the father of the woman Josh was in love with. At that time, she had not even met Jerilyn.

She couldn't help laughing. Thinking about Jefferson, there was almost the giddiness of a young girl with a crush on some schoolboy.

~

The plane was in the air, Jeff on his way back to KC and home in OP. From the time he woke up, he had kept busy, getting ready for his return trip. No time to think about the previous days.

Now, his mind returned to those last few minutes with Martie, the words she spoke and his words in answer. Neither had expected to voice their suppressed feelings, even though there had finally been kisses. But could anything come from those deeper feelings?

~

Jeff leaned back in the seat and closed his eyes, thinking of Martie, remembering their words and their kisses. A smile spread across his face. *Ah, Martie, I'm so glad we met, but we live so far apart. Will that ever change? Is there any way that it could?*

He fell asleep—dreaming about that special woman in Nebraska. The flight attendant woke him to let him know they would soon be landing. He tried to remember what his dream was about. He wasn't looking forward to going home, to what might, probably would be an empty house. Even when Jon was off, he was often with Linda if she was in town.

Why didn't I have someone else bring me to the airport and pick me up? One of the old cops probably would have been glad to do so. As he was driving home, he thought, *I need to get used to this anyway. Jon is soon going to be married and not in my house even when he's off.*

～

Before he left for the trip to Nebraska, Jeff had given both his sons his flight schedules. He had been home only a short time when Jack called.

"Hey, Dad, how was your trip? How's my sister?"

"It was a good trip. Your sister's okay."

Jack could almost feel his dad's fatigue. "Good. It's probably been a long day for you. Jayden and I wondered if we could pick up some food and come share it with you.

"Maybe we could visit awhile, learn how everything is in Nebraska."

"Oh, Son. That all sounds good," Jeff told him.

"Great! Anything special you would like?"

"No. Whatever will be perfect and greatly appreciated."

~

Jeff took his luggage into his bedroom and left it. He was exhausted, just as Jack had sensed, and thought, *I might wait till morning to unpack.* When he returned to the living room, he collapsed into the reclining chair Jerilyn and Josh had given him for Christmas.

~

In Nebraska, the day had seemed extra-long for Martie, one with no time or communication with Jefferson. She didn't know what time he would get home, but decided to send a text anyway. If he was there, maybe he would call.

Dear Jefferson, It's been a long day here. Hope it's been a safe day for you. If you're home, maybe you can give me a call? She closed it with *Love* and a heart emoji.

Martie was disappointed she didn't hear from him. Maybe he wasn't home yet. She still hoped to hear from him before bedtime, so when the phone rang, her heart started beating faster, then she saw it was Josh. Her son texted more often than he called, so she was concerned. Had something happened? There must be some reason for his calling.

"Josh?"

"Mom. You sound concerned, any reason?"

She told him, "No. I first thought the call might be from Jefferson. I sent a text to him, haven't heard back. And you usually text."

"Oh, sorry to worry you," Josh said. "I just want to check, see how you are. Jerilyn and I couldn't miss how you and Jeff enjoy being together. And now, you'll be separated again. Wanted to let you know we love you, want to make sure you're okay."

Martie said, "I love you both too. Thank you for checking. I'm okay, or will be, have to be."

Josh told her, "Be sure to let us know if we can help with any-thing." He laughed and added, "Though I don't know what it would be. Bye, Mom."

"Bye, Josh. I will let you know if there's anything you can do for me."

Twenty-Six

Just as Jack rang the doorbell, Jefferson noticed that Martie had texted him. He invited his son and daughter-in-law in, then read the text. *Yes, I will definitely call her, but not until the kids have left. I want to feel free and open when I talk to that special lady.*

Jack placed the food on the table where Jeff already had plates and silverware, then both he and Jayden hugged his dad. Jeff asked the young couple what they would like to drink. They surprised him when they asked if he had any tea, telling him that hot tea would go well with what they had brought.

He gave them a wondering look, then went to check through the cabinets. "I'm sure you probably know I don't drink it often, but I happen to have some special tea. I'll get cups, then heat up the water."

Jack and Jayden smiled at each other as they started placing the food on the table. What might Jeff think of their choice? He had filled the teakettle, turned the burner on, and as they expected, eyed the food with almost suspicion.

"Okay. You have whetted my curiosity, what is it?"

"Well, you know there've been quite a few changes in downtown OP, including adding new eating places.

"This is Thai food from Lulu's. It's on Santa Fe, about halfway between Seventy-Ninth and Eightieth Streets. We've eaten there several times and really like it. Hope you will too. If not, guess we'll have to think of something else."

The tea was ready to drink and Jeff put the cups on the table. He served himself from the food as Jack and Jayden had done already. Before their first bite, Jack said, "Let's give thanks."

The three bowed their heads as he prayed. "Father, we thank You for Dad's safe trip and return home. We thank You for all Your blessings, including this food. In Jesus' name, we pray." All said, "Amen."

Jack and Jayden waited for Jeff to take his first bites, watching for his response. Noticing their attention, he said, "I like it, a good choice."

They all smiled, and after they all started their meal, Jayden asked, "How are Jerilyn and Josh?"

Jack added, "And Martie."

Jeff took a sip of his tea, then told them, "They are all doing okay. I went to school one day with Josh and Jerilyn, talked to their students about my police career. That was interesting. I was surprised at all the questions from the kids."

Jayden asked, though she knew the answer, "Did you spend any time with Josh's mother?"

Her father-in-law took several more bites before answering. "We visited the ranch the Wilsons had owned, where Josh and his sister grew up. The people who own it now took us on a tour, and we drove by the farm where she grew up."

The young couple knew there had been more but chose not to mention it. There would be another wedding in Overland Park in just a few weeks. They would wait to see what might happen then.

Jeff said, "I have to tell you, this meal has been a surprise. I like it. Would either of you like some more tea?"

"Yes," from both Jack and Jayden.

They had their second helping, helped Jeff clean up the kitchen, then told him they needed to get back home. There were hugs again when they left and said, "It's been a good evening. Love you."

Jeff waved as they backed out of the driveway, closed and locked the door, then picked up his phone. It was time to call Martie. He didn't want to wait any longer to hear her voice.

~

After the phone call from her son, Martie thought, *I need to eat something anyway, but what?* Checking the cabinets and refrigerator, she saw nothing that appealed to her. She finally decided to make an omelet and toast. Maybe it would fill the emptiness she was feeling.

There was a phone call just as she took her last bite. When she saw it was Jefferson, there was the extra heartbeat that had come to be usual.

"Hello."

"It's Jefferson."

"Yes."

"I would have called sooner, but Jack and Jayden came by with food. I wanted to wait until it was just me," he told her.

"Brought food, huh? How did that come to be?"

Jefferson said, "I had given the boys my flight schedule, so Jack knew when I would probably be home. He and Jayden correctly anticipated I would be hungry as well as weary. I was home only a short while when he called and asked if they could bring something."

Martie said, "That's thoughtful. What did they bring?"

"It was Thai food from a restaurant in Overland Park, fairly new. I had never eaten there. It was good, different, spicy; I liked it. There were even fortune rolls for each of us."

"Fortune rolls, that sounds interesting. Like Chinese fortune cookies?"

"Yeah."

"So did you get an interesting fortune?"

Jeff didn't answer for a while, then said, "You might think so. It said, 'Love is a game that two can play and both win'."

"Yes, it is."

Continuing with a description of the meal, he told her, "The kids said the appropriate drink to have with it was hot tea. I happened to have some tea bags, not the same flavor as offered at Lulu's, but it served the purpose.

"How has your day been?"

"It seemed extra long," Martie told him. "Checked my flower beds, but they are in pretty good shape. I didn't know the times of your flight—when you left here and landed at KCI. Felt lost."

"Yeah, I was sad I had to leave. Sorry I didn't let you know when I got home. Think I told you I would."

"Yes, you did."

"When I was driving home, I was feeling sad," Jeff said. "Wished I had asked someone to take me to the airport and pick me up; I was pretty tired. After Jack called, I collapsed in my recliner.

"I noticed your text just as Jack and Jayden got here. And like I said, wanted to wait till I was alone to answer it. Sorry it took so long."

"I forgive you. So glad to talk to you; just wish you weren't so far away."

"Me, too."

Martie and Jefferson were both quiet, remembering the cherished, memorable occasions when they were recently together and the words they had exchanged.

Finally, Martie asked, "Do you have anything planned for the rest of the week?"

"No, but wondering if I might be able to spend special time with Jon. It's just a few weeks till he's married."

"I was glad Nancy and I made sure to do that, even before she got engaged," Martie told him. "Those times had tapered off since she settled in Scottsbluff. It was almost like getting reacquainted."

Quiet again, then a question from Jefferson, "So will you be here for the wedding?"

"I hope so."

"I do too," he admitted. "Guess I don't really have any news. Glad we got to talk."

"Yes. Maybe I'll call tomorrow."

Jefferson told her, "I'll look forward to it," and unexpectedly said, "Love you. Bye."

"You too. Bye."

Still holding his phone, Jeff's mind returned to his, "Love you." The words had come almost automatically, and Martie had answered, "You too." It was as if they had been in their minds a long time—certainly before they first voiced them that time at Martie's.

Twenty-Seven

A few days later, when Jon was off, he and Jeff were having breakfast. His dad said, "The days are really rushing toward the day you get married. And, I'm thinking also, the day when we will have less time to spend together. It's been too easy to let chances pass, maybe even waste the opportunity.

"Anyway, I know you're rightly busy with important things, but I'd still like to have that special occasion with you."

"Me, too, Dad."

Jeff said, "You told me you and Linda had chosen which of the Chief's houses you're going to rent. How are you doing regarding furniture?"

"We've picked out a few things Chief Brooks saved from what past renters left. There's enough to start with. I'm going to move my bed there in the next few days."

"Guess that means you won't be living here after that," Jeff noted, almost sadly.

"I'm sorry. Yes, I guess it does. Linda and I plan to go shopping for whatever else we need when we're home from our honeymoon. Would you like to see it?"

His dad told him, "Yes, I would. You probably know I've been curious, not that it's any of my business."

Jon reached his arm around his dad's shoulder and said, "It's okay; maybe a good thing to be curious, make sure all is well."

Jeff laughed and said, "If you say so."

"Okay, so, how about now? Do you have plans, anything you have to do?"

"No," his dad said. "Except maybe getting groceries."

Jon asked, "How about we go tour the house, then stop by the store before coming back here?"

"That's a plan. Will be good to have someone with me, maybe choose something new. I get in a rut, getting the same things every week."

"Might be good practice for me," Jon said. "I sure haven't made any lists for a trip to the grocery store."

～

Jeff made note of the neighborhoods they drove through to get to the house where Jon and Linda would live. He remembered patrolling through the same ones when he was on the Overland Park Police Department, could almost picture some incidents that had resulted in his being dispatched.

Jon noticed how his dad had become quiet, almost reflective, wondering about the reason. He pulled into the driveway at what would be his home, parked, and turned off the engine. Jeff was still looking around, and he asked, "Anything wrong?"

"No," his dad told him. "Just recalling the days when I was on the police force and patrolled this area."

"Ah, any specific memories? Were there problems you had to take care of?"

Jeff told him, "I vaguely remember being dispatched for a few minor problems, but mostly all the areas we drove through were quiet and friendly, good places to raise a family."

At hearing the words *raising a family* Jon became quiet. He hadn't thought of that possibility when he and Linda were choosing a house to live in. How long might they live in this house? Would they have a family? Her sister had two children now, and he knew Linda loved her nephew and niece.

Now his sister was pregnant, and though they hadn't said anything specific, he knew Jack loved Jayden's niece and nephews almost as much as she did. Probably kids in the future for them.

"Jon."

"Huh? Oh, sorry, Dad. Just pondering. Your mention of raising a family made me realize I haven't considered that possibility. I do like kids but hadn't thought I might be a daddy someday."

Jeff glanced at his son and noticed his pensive smile. Then Jon said, "I brought you here to see the house, so let's go in."

When they were inside with Jon showing his dad around, he looked at all the rooms in a different way, as if there were children living in them, playing and running around.

"It all looks great," Jeff told him. "In good shape. Guess everything works?"

"Yeah. A little fixing up was needed and the Chief just finished that."

There was a small table with two chairs in the kitchen, and Jon asked his dad, "Would you like to rest awhile? Except, no dishes yet, and I can't even offer you a glass of water."

Jeff smiled and said, "Thank you, but I'll wait till you move in."

"Good idea. So, anything else you want to see?"

"Think I've seen everything. Are you ready to go grocery shopping?"

~

When they were back at Jeff's, putting groceries away, Jon asked, "So, Dad, did you and Mom talk about having a family before you got married?"

Jeff was getting ready to put cans of soup in the cabinet, but stopped at his son's query, giving him a quizzical look.

"Why the question?"

"You said something about the area where Linda and I are going to live being good for raising a family. We haven't talked about that, so wondered if you did."

"Not that I remember, but we did both like kids."

"Yeah, we do too."

~

At the store, Jon had purchased some items too, and now asked, "Is it okay if I just leave these in your cabinet for now? Maybe I'll get a few more things to take to my house next time I go."

"Yes, of course."

~

When he was at the house with his dad, Jon realized that, in addition to having no food, there were also no dishes, pots and pans, or cooking utensils and silverware. Thankfully, there were some things at Jeff's he could take. Linda checked with her mom, who provided more. So there was enough for them and even a few extra dishes and silverware, should they have company. That meant when

Jon took his bed and the groceries he had purchased, he could prepare meals for himself.

When Linda was away, Jon was surprised how lonely he felt when he wasn't on duty and only him in the house, though that would be true until his wedding. How might his dad feel? In all the years since his mother died, he and Jack were living there, at least until he got married in December. *Now I'm gone and soon to be married myself.*

He recalled the question from Pastor Bradley when he met with him about performing the marriage service. He had noted how Jeff and Martie Wilson enjoyed being together at Jerilyn's wedding and Jon told him she would be invited to his. *All three of you Tates will have been married in less than a year. Since your dad will be living alone, might he want to get married too?*

Linda had asked Jon the same thing, "Have you ever thought your dad might want to be married again?"

Would he, or anyone, want to be married again, just so they wouldn't be alone? *I don't believe that would be true of Dad.* But, considering those questions and remembering how Jeff and Martie seemed to be happy together, especially those days after Jack's wedding and before Christmas, made Jon think, *Maybe he might be in love again and want to be married. I wonder what he would say if I asked him.*

I could ask Jerilyn. Dad was with them for a week when he went for Josh's sister's wedding. I'm sure there were times when he and Martie were together in addition to being at the wedding. Still, after a little more contemplation, he chose not to. Whatever would be with them, would be, and eventually, everyone would know.

∾

Jeff knew his children speculated about his relationship with Martie and what might come of it, Jerilyn most of all. She and Josh had seen their kisses. But she couldn't have known how they made him feel. Then there were the words from Martie, "I think I love you." He admitted that he felt the same.

Neither had expected to ever feel that again. For him, that created a certain feeling of guilt. Maybe for Martie too. Both had been so in love with their mate, and though they had confessed their love to each other, they weren't sure what could come of it, somehow feeling their circumstance was different than that of Josh and Jerilyn.

Jeff's daughter lived in the same town as her mother-in-law. If he visited Jerilyn, he could see Martie. But just seeing wouldn't be enough. Jeff continued his thoughts. *Well, there will be another wedding here in Overland Park in just a few weeks, and Martie is coming.*

Knowing he would see her, be with her soon, produced that extra heartbeat that still surprised him. He wasn't aware of the contemplative smile that appeared when he thought of Martie—and it did often.

~

The time for Jon's and Linda's wedding was passing quickly, though it didn't seem so for them, probably because he was still fulfilling all of his shifts and she had several flights, leaving only a few days, seemingly hours, for them to complete all their plans.

Jefferson and Martie were often in touch, and phone calls had become their main communication. It was a rare day they didn't talk, and with another wedding scheduled, they expected to see each other and be together again soon.

With only days before that special day, Jeff said, "We haven't talked about when you will arrive. Jerilyn and Josh are staying here, though we haven't talked about time."

Martie didn't answer his question, but told him, "They first talked about driving, since school is out, they have time to do so. But because of her pregnancy, decided it would be better to fly. I believe they are planning to go a few days early so they can spend more time with you."

"So, are you coming with them? When is your flight? How long will you be here? Since Josh and Jerilyn plan to stay with me, I hope you are too. There's a bit more room now, since Jon has moved out."

One couldn't miss how happy Jeff was that he would soon see Martie again and hopefully have her staying in his house. His words almost ran together.

There was no answer for a while, then Martie told him, "I'm sorry, I'm not. I didn't know they were going early, so when Nancy asked if they could make flight arrangements for me, as well as reserve a room at the hotel, I agreed.

"I kind of enjoy having my kids take responsibility for me at times. Because of ranch obligations, they are more limited on time, so we will come late Thursday and leave early Sunday afternoon."

"Oh."

Martie could almost feel Jefferson's letdown. In previous calls, there was a certain eagerness in them both as they discussed the upcoming time.

"I'm sorry, and disappointed, too, that we won't have as much time together as we hoped."

A bit more silence, then, "Maybe you can change your return flight, move here from the hotel, then fly back with Jerilyn and Josh?

"Martie?"

"Sorry. Before any of us made plans for our trip, Jerilyn and I did talk about my staying with you—well—along with them. If anyone besides you and me have any idea of our feelings for each other, she does."

"Yeah," Jefferson agreed. "She and Josh even witnessed our kiss." He sounded amused and happy as he voiced the thought. "So?"

"Okay."

"You said okay?"

"Yes," Martie sounded happier with her answer.

Twenty-Eight

Jeff stepped into the room that had been Jon's and the one that would be Martie's when she came. He realized he had been so excited, knowing she would be in his house again, that he had forgotten an important fact—no bed. So, a decision to be made, buy a new bed or something different, maybe a daybed.

He had never been responsible for choosing furniture. He and Joyce made those decisions together. Though, for the most part, final selections were always hers. *It would be good to have someone advise me about the best choice.*

At another time or circumstance, that might be Martie, instead, *I need to talk to Jerilyn anyway. I'll ask her what she thinks.*

"Dad. You usually text, but glad to hear your voice."

"Yes, yours, too. How are your days? How are you feeling?"

Jerilyn told him, "Glad to have some leisure time. And for the most part, feeling good. Looking forward to seeing you soon. Have we given you our schedule for the trip?"

"No, you haven't," Jeff said. "Would probably be good to know. Martie told me you're coming a day early."

"Yes. We have the time, so thought it would be good to spend more time with you. We'll get there Wednesday and stay till Tuesday. Hope that's okay with you.

"Did Martie tell you she's coming with Nancy and Mitchell?"

Her dad told her, "Yes, she did. I asked her if she could change her return flight to the same as yours, leave the hotel and come spend the rest of the time here.

"That's one reason I'm calling. I need some advice. Jon moved his bed and dresser to his house. I need to get a new bed, or maybe a daybed for that room. What do you think?"

"Oh. I hadn't even thought about that."

Jerilyn was quiet for a while as if thinking, then, "I vote for a daybed. It could be the beginning of furnishing a unique room, not necessarily a bedroom.

"You need to decide whether you want to keep it a bedroom. Guess that could still be true with a daybed. For some reason, in my mind, a daybed would make it more distinctive, definitely a guest room, not that a bedroom can't fill that purpose temporarily."

"Thanks. Whatever I decide, there's not much time to take care of it. Wish you were here to go shopping with me."

Jerilyn assured him, "I do too, Dad. I'll be anxious to see the room when we're there."

~

Jon and Jack were both off duty the day their dad went shopping, so the three went together to check out furniture. After looking at what was available, they decided on a daybed, thinking it could be the beginning of converting the room into a warm, inviting space.

The boys both voiced their feeling that their mother would have loved the transformation. Glancing at his dad, Jon said, "I bet Martie will like it too."

~

Jeff stepped into the 'new guest room,' wanting to double check, making sure all was as it should be, or at least what he hoped it would be. It was Wednesday and not long before Jerilyn and Josh would be there. They wouldn't be using this room, but he knew Jerilyn would want to make a thorough check.

When he shopped for groceries earlier in the day, he had been sure to get extra, though not sure what meals might be prepared in his kitchen. He wanted to be ready, just in case. For today, he expected to have something delivered so no one would have to leave once they were settled in.

Martie had called earlier. They were both disappointed she wasn't coming with their kids but agreed it was probably a good thing. Jeff would have that extra time with them, Jerilyn especially, more than when he was in Plattsford for Nancy's wedding.

There would be more time to visit, talk about the coming grandchild, pondering about whether it would be a boy or a girl and what name might they choose.

Jeff wondered if it was an anomaly that he was so excited about being a grandfather. *Is that a normal thing for a man?*

When Jerilyn and Josh arrived, the thought of his coming grandchild was still on Jeff's mind. He greeted them both with hugs. There were tears in his eyes when he told them, "I'm so glad to see you."

The two young people hugged him back, unsure of his emotional greeting but happy to wrap themselves in his love.

Jerilyn told him, "We're glad to see you, too, Dad. Though it hasn't been that long since you were with us. It will be good to get caught up on everything.

"So, do we have the same room?" she asked, smiling.

Smiling himself, Jeff told her, "Yes, you know the way. When you're settled, come to the kitchen. We can have coffee if you want and decide what to order for supper."

When she got to the kitchen, Jerilyn told her dad, "I'm limiting coffee to one cup a day until Baby is here. I'll have water, please, or maybe juice if you have some."

Jeff said, "It's been a long time. I had forgotten about that need for an expectant mom to watch what she ate."

Jerilyn couldn't miss the tender, poignant smile on her dad's face. Had it been there before, even when she still lived in Overland Park and she missed it? Seeing it reinforced hers and Josh's decision that it had been good to come early.

~

They were at the kitchen table with their coffee and juice when Jeff asked, "Do you have anything in mind for our meal?"

After some discussion, they decided to order from Cheddars. Jerilyn and her dad both had a favorite. Josh had never eaten there, but checking the online menu, chose one that looked good.

Jerilyn told the two men, "It's going to be awhile before you order and more time before the food is delivered, so I hope you'll excuse me. I need a nap." She kissed her husband, and as she headed toward the bedroom, told him, "If I'm still asleep, wake me when the food arrives."

When Jerilyn left for her nap, it was as if Jeff and Josh weren't sure what to do with their time. Finally, Josh asked, "So, what's been keeping you busy since Nancy's wedding, besides buying new furniture?"

"Not much more than the usual everyday things," Jeff told him. "Jon did take me for a tour of the house where he and Linda will live. It was interesting driving through the neighborhood— one I regularly patrolled when I was a police officer."

Checking the time, he said, "Guess we should order our meal. We'll be ready to eat when it arrives."

His words were as much to change the subject as anything. The only other thing he could remember spending time on was talking to Martie—often.

Josh agreed and grinned. He knew from visiting with his mom that she was talking with Jefferson—often. Pondering that, he admitted that it was a good thing, having the man as his father-in-law. *He might even be my stepfather someday.*

Jeff wondered at his son-in-law's smile. What might be going through his mind?

Josh had contemplated what the changes in relationship could lead to if his mother and Jeff should marry. He and Jerilyn would be stepbrother and stepsister. Wasn't that something to consider? *I wonder if Mom and Jeff have thought about that.*

~

Jerilyn came out of the bedroom, and Jeff asked if she had gotten the rest she needed. She had gone to her husband, given him a kiss, then told her dad, "I did, and I'm hungry. Is the food here yet?"

The doorbell rang just as she finished the question. Her dad smiled and said, "Yes!" He had set the table while they waited, and glasses of water were at each place. Josh went to the door to get their food and carried it to the kitchen, setting it on the countertop where each of them could get theirs and take to the table.

Besides their meal, there were the honey butter croissants. Jeff and Jerilyn had forgotten they were always a part of the meal at the restaurant. It was all new to Josh, but he was ready to try them.

The container holding the croissants was set in the middle of the table, then the three picked up their meals and took them to the place they would sit. They bowed their heads while Jeff said grace, then each took their first bite, Jerilyn and her dad keeping their eyes on Josh, wondering if he would be happy with what he had chosen.

He noticed and said, "I like it. Wonder if there are any Cheddars restaurants in Nebraska? Always good to have a new place to go."

When they were finished with the meal and everything cleaned up, Jerilyn said, "I'd like to see the new room," and headed that way with Josh and Jeff following.

"Oh, I like it, Dad. You and the boys chose well."

"Yeah. Even had to get some special sheets and pillows and a bed cover. Never thought of everything someone has to consider when they get new furniture."

Jerilyn was looking around the room with a questioning look. Her dad told her, "Yes, Jon took the dresser, too, so need to get one, or something more fitting for the room."

He pointed out the mirror on the inside of the closet door. "This will have to suffice for now."

"Since we're going to be here, maybe we can all go shopping Monday," Jerilyn suggested. Continuing with that thought, she said, "Martie might have some good ideas after spending time in the room."

Her eyes were on her dad when she completed voicing the idea. She could tell he agreed with her even though he said nothing.

Josh was looking back and forth between his wife and his father-in-law. *Yeah, Mom would like that.*

Finally, Jeff said, "Guess we'll have to wait and see."

Twenty-Nine

artie had called earlier, before Josh and Jerilyn arrived. Jeff was glad to have had that time to visit. Phone visits had become their main method of communication, though texts and emails were good when they thought of something more they wanted to share or if they might have questions.

Now that it was the end of the day, after the few hours with their kids, Jeff was thinking, *I need to tell Martie about our day, ask her what she did, if she's ready for her trip. I'll send a text later.*

The three were relaxed in the living room when Jeff asked the expectant parents if they were still waiting to learn the gender of their child and, "Are you considering names?"

Josh told him, "Guess it would be easier if we knew whether Baby is going to be a boy or a girl. Yeah, we've talked about names, some serious, some just for fun.

"We're so used to calling 'it' Baby, we might continue that after the birth."

Jerilyn added, "At least Baby fits both. We've decided we don't want a Junior if it's a boy. Besides, that's another J and we think there are enough J's in the family already. It seems to have become a practice for girls to be given their mother's maiden name, can't think of any that would work with Tate, maybe Tattoo, or Tatania, or Tatia?"

Then she asked her dad, "Do you have any ideas? What about when you and mom chose names for us kids?"

"No ideas," Jeff told her. "Except for your name. You've heard that story. Can't say I remember how or why we settled on the names for your brothers."

"We do have awhile longer," Jerilyn admitted. "One of the teachers at our school told me that she and her husband had picked out a name for their baby, then when she was born, they decided it didn't fit and chose another one."

Her dad told her, "If I think of any, I'll let you know."

The three spent a bit more time discussing the future with a baby in the picture. Jeff couldn't help the grin on his face as he imagined what that would be like. He and Jerilyn talked about past times, which Josh also enjoyed, learning more about the family of the woman he loved.

But it wasn't long before Jerilyn said, "I've enjoyed this time so much and hate to interrupt, but I need to call it a day."

She went to her dad to give him a hug and confessed, "I can't remember any time we have reminisced so much. It's been wonderful. I love you, Dad."

"I love you too. Seems like it's taken being separated to appreciate those things. Do you want me to wake you up in the morning or just let you get up when you're ready?"

"Tomorrow will be the last time we can just relax, not have to watch the clock. Guess I'm saying we'll get up when we get up," Jerilyn said with a smile.

Jeff told her, "Sounds good to me. Hope you sleep well and get a good rest," giving her a hug at the door to the room that would be hers and Josh's while they were there.

He turned out lights and went to his room, taking his phone out of his pocket to give Martie a call.

"Hello, Jefferson."

"Hello, Martie."

"I wondered if you might call again. Guess the kids got there okay?"

"They did," Jeff told her. "We had meals delivered so we'd have more time to visit."

Martie asked, "Did you talk about the baby?"

"Of course. Mostly about what the name might be. Jerilyn asked how it was when her mom and I chose names. She knows the story about hers, but I don't remember how or why her brothers got the names they did."

Martie told him, "Josh told me about Jerilyn's name."

"How about your kids?" Jeff asked her.

"Josh—Joshua—Samuel was named for his grandfathers. My dad was Joshua and Andrew's dad was Samuel.

"Nancy's middle name is the same as mine, Elizabeth. Nancy was the name of a favorite aunt. Guess we weren't very inventive," she admitted.

They were quiet for a while, each thinking their conversation could have been that of an old married couple.

Martie changed the subject by asking, "So you enjoyed the day?"

"I did. Wish you had been here."

"Me too." What do you have planned for tomorrow?"

He realized he had given no thought to what they might do to occupy their time, so said, "Don't know. Guess we'll decide in the morning. Jack and Jayden did invite us for supper, so I won't have to cook. Think they're curious to see what Jerilyn might feel about being a guest in the home that had been hers.

"What about you?"

Martie told him, "I'll be making sure I have what I need for the wedding, and afterward, make sure I have enough clothes, and getting them packed." She was remembering Jack's wedding when she was at Jefferson's house longer than she had expected to be.

"Guess there's nothing else. Need to get to bed so I'll be ready for whatever tomorrow brings. Glad we got to talk again. Look forward to seeing you soon."

"Me too," Martie agreed, then before telling him bye, told him, "Love you."

"Love you." They said, "Bye," together.

Before he fell asleep, Jeff's mind turned to what he and Jerilyn and Josh might do to occupy their time the next day, beyond visiting and more catching up. There were a lot of new businesses in old downtown Overland Park that might interest Jerilyn. *Probably me too*, Jeff admitted to himself. Some of those businesses were cafés or restaurants, which could solve the problem of *What's for lunch?* and *Where will it be?*

On Thursday, Jeff, Jerilyn, and Josh spent the morning visiting stores in Overland Park, some recently established and others with different businesses than in the past, all new to all of them. Instead of choosing one of the new places, they had lunch at Dragon Inn; it was a favorite of Jerilyn's, who said, "We can eat at one of the others another time."

After lunch, the couple wanted to visit a place that was special to them, the Arboretum. Josh said, "I enjoyed being there but kept my eye out for an appropriate place to propose, so missed a lot."

They invited Jeff to join them, but he chose to stay home. When the kids left and he was alone, his thoughts were on Martie. *I'd like to call her, but she's probably already on the plane. Wish I could see her before the rehearsal tomorrow. Maybe she'll call when she's settled at the hotel, or at least send a text.*

~

Thursday morning, Martie was ready to be picked up by Nancy and Mitchell for the trip to the airport, anxious to be on the way to Overland Park, Kansas. She thought back to the day before when she had last talked to Jefferson, telling him she was making sure she had enough clothes for the wedding and every other possible event.

There had been several outfits spread on her bed. The only sure thing was her dress for the wedding, but she wondered, *Do I need anything else that's dressy? What about church?* Her usual attire for that was pants, and she had noticed that was also true of the women at Jeff's church when she was there. She wanted to have enough, *but do I have too much?*

She had made her final decisions and packed her suitcases but waited to close them up until Thursday morning, confident she had all she would need.

~

Jerilyn needed a nap after the trip to the Arboretum, and there was time for one as Jack and Jayden had said supper would be ready at 6:00.

She had mixed feelings about visiting in the house that had been hers for several years. Though she was more curious than anything else, wondering about any changes, if there might be a different ambience. It had been the home of a single female, now the occupants included her brother Jack. And Jerilyn didn't miss it, she loved her home and the house she lived in with Josh.

All three—Jeff, Jerilyn, and Josh—were greeted with smiles and hugs when they got there. Everyone was glad to see all the others. Jack said, "Supper's ready. Come in, find a seat."

When they were settled, he asked his dad to say grace. All bowed their heads and Jeff prayed, "Father, we thank You for this special time when we can be together to share our love and time. Bless this food to our bodies. Amen."

Jack said to Jerilyn, "Sis, I came here a lot to have a meal with you. Kind of neat to have you here for a meal with me."

"And it's so good to be here with both of you," Jerilyn told him and Jayden. "And the food is so good. So, who prepared it?"

Jayden said, "Actually, we both did. Jack prepared the brisket when he was off. The rest of it didn't really take much time or effort. In fact, I have to admit that I used a packaged mix for the mashed potatoes, just had to add boiling water.

"There's peach cobbler for dessert if anyone wants it."

Seeing the questioning look on Jeff's face, she told them, "I made it. It's been in the freezer, just had to warm it up."

With a smile, Jack said, "I voted for brownies, but she overruled me." He had come to Jayden, wrapped her in his arms for a hug, then gave her a kiss.

Jayden explained, "When we first got together, we learned that we both seemed to be addicted to them, and I baked them often."

When they finished the meal, all of them worked together to clean up. Then Jack asked his sister, "Want a tour?"

"You know I do."

Jack led with his sister beside him while Jayden, Josh, and Jeff followed. When they finished, he asked, "So what do you think?"

Jerilyn took his hand and said, "I think it's all your and Jayden's home now. I can feel your personalities and the love that fills it."

They were in the living room, still visiting when Jeff received a text. Jerilyn, seeing his smile, guessed it was from her mother-in-law. She even asked, "Martie?"

"Yes." He stepped away from the group to read it, then told them, "They're in OP, at the hotel."

He moved back into the kitchen to send a reply. *"So glad to learn you're here. We're still at Jack's; wish you could have been with us. Will be so glad to see you tomorrow. We may be too busy with wedding things to talk or text before rehearsal, but would love to hear your voice. Love."*

Thirty

As they expected, there was little time to do so, but Jefferson and Martie were able to have a couple of short phone calls and finally, to meet at the church before rehearsal started. No one could miss how glad they were to see each other, to be together. With happy smiles, they moved toward each other, and in spite of the presence of everyone else, hugged. Though they both wanted a kiss, they refrained, waiting for a time when there was not such a crowd.

When Jeff was in Plattsford for Nancy Wilson's wedding, Josh and Jerilyn had witnessed the growing affection their parents had for each other. Though they had shared that information with her brothers, Jack and Jon were still surprised. No question their dad cared very much for their sister's mother-in-law. The two were usually hand in hand and loath to separate at the end of the evening.

But what can come from it? They're older, live far apart, not easy to get together, though Jerilyn and Josh did. If they care as much for each other as seems evident, might they want to be married, be together always? One of them would have to move. How would they decide? Probably more complicated than for our sister and Josh.

~

The next day, Jeff and Martie were seated together as they had been at other weddings. Many of the guests had seen that, so no one thought that there might be more than friendship between them, though Linda's parents sensed a subtle difference. Not everyone could see, but their hands were clasped together. Occasionally, their heads leaned toward the other, a slight touch, then a smile.

As before at the reception, they were glad to take advantage of the dancing, the opportunity to wrap their arms around the other. Some of Jeff's friends who had witnessed that after Jerilyn's wedding almost a year before were sure the two were holding each other closer.

When it was time to toss the bouquet, some even wondered if Martie might join the group. She didn't, but was holding hands with Jeff, and they turned to each other with smiles when they saw Deena Edmonds catch it and how happy she was. She had been dating Jon's firefighter friend, Garrett Allen, the one he had helped put up Christmas lights. It seemed like their relationship was serious.

~

Jefferson drove Martie back to the hotel and rode in the elevator with her to her floor, then to her room. During the evening, they had held hands and hugged, but there had been no kiss, which they both wanted. As soon as they were in the room and the door closed, they fulfilled that desire, each of them still in wonder at the love they felt.

They leaned back, arms still around each other, smiled, then a hug, and another quick kiss. Jeff said, "I'm so glad you're here."

"Me too," Martie told him. "Guess we need to talk about plans for tomorrow and the rest of the time I'm here."

They both took seats, then Jeff said, "I figured I would pick you up tomorrow morning for church."

Martie nodded her head in agreement.

"So do you want to check out and bring your luggage then or wait until after lunch?"

"I'm not sure what time checkout is, but if I can, would rather come back to get it later."

Martie was sitting on the couch, Jefferson in another chair. At her words, he rose, came to sit beside her, and took her hand. "That sounds good to me; you wouldn't have to rush. Whatever you find out, call me. If you need to leave earlier, I'll come early to help you before church."

Then he stood, pulling her up beside him, and said, "Now, guess I better leave so we can both get a good night's sleep."

They walked hand in hand to the door, their arms went around each other almost automatically, then a goodnight kiss.

"Love you," Jefferson told her.

"And I love you," from Martie.

~

Martie learned she could check out at two o'clock, meaning Jefferson didn't need to arrive early. But he did, and she was glad to see him, eager for the kiss he greeted her with.

Martie told him, "I'm pretty much ready for checkout; it won't take long to finish. What are we going to do the rest of the day?"

Even though it was early, Jefferson took her hand to lead her to the door and told her, "First, lunch after church, then back here to

pick up your things." As they walked toward the elevator, he continued, "We can decide together what to do after that."

Their children arrived at church the same time they did, and they
sat in the same row, Josh and Jerilyn, Jefferson and Martie, then Jack
and Jayden. Though they were seated between their children, the
older couple held hands throughout the service.

~

Jack had been off Friday and Saturday, so he was able to be
included in his brother's wedding. Back to work for him Sunday
afternoon after the group had lunch together. Not knowing whether
he would see them again before they left, he and Jayden lingered
briefly to visit just a bit more with Jerilyn, Josh, and Martie.

"Good to be with you again, Sis," Jack told her. "Still miss our
times together, kind of surprises me, never thought there would
come a time we'd live in different parts of the country."

Josh said, "Well, it's not that far away, don't have to travel across
the ocean. You and Jayden need to come visit, see where we live."

There were hugs all around between the young couples as well as
Martie. And there were tears.

"We'll check the calendar," Jayden told them, "see what's coming
up. If not before, maybe we'll come see the baby?"

More hugs, then, though reluctant to leave, Jack and Jayden separated from the group. Most Sundays, she would have gone to her
office during second service to see if there was anything she needed
to address. Because of the wedding, someone else had taken that
responsibility. Jack would have just enough time to change and head
to the PD after they got home.

Jerilyn needed a nap, so she and Josh were on their way back to her dad's house. Jefferson and Martie would get her things from the hotel then head back there too.

~

Martie knew about the recent purchase of the daybed for the room she would use. She was anxious to see it and perhaps consider another furniture piece to complete the ambience as Jerilyn had suggested. She had also hinted that maybe Martie and her dad could go shopping for such the next day.

Jefferson carried Martie's luggage into the room and watched her as she looked around then sat on the bed. *Ah, comfortable*, she thought. She wanted to lie down, learn what it might be like to sleep on it, but not with Jefferson watching.

He had set the bags down and showed her where the bed linens were. "Do you want me to make it up for you?"

"How about we do it together?" she asked.

That's what they did with much laughing and fussing about the process. When they finished, Jefferson asked, "Want to try it out?" Then wondered, *Why did I ask that?*

She flushed at the thought, lying on the bed with Jefferson watching, but said only, "I'll wait."

Still, they smiled, hugged, then left the room at the same time Josh and Jerilyn came out of their room, all of them ending up in the living room. Jerilyn had said she needed a nap, and Josh told his mom and Jeff he had taken one too. All four took seats, Jeff and Martie on the couch holding hands.

Jerilyn said, "Martie, guess you saw the daybed. What do you think? Isn't it cute?"

"Yes, I like it," Martie replied. "Very comfortable. I guess it is cute."

When she mentioned it being comfortable, both Josh and Jerilyn wondered what that implied, glancing at each other with questions on their faces. Jefferson and Martie noted that and turned to each other with smiles, having an idea what was on their children's minds.

Dismissing for now the questions in her mind, Jerilyn asked, "Do you plan to go shopping for another piece?"

Jeff told her, "We'll decide tomorrow. What about you and Josh?"

"We haven't decided what we're going to do either," Josh told him.

With no other plans, the four spent the afternoon sharing histories and anecdotes about their families. Jerilyn and Josh heard things they didn't know or didn't remember. Martie and Josh were glad to learn more about the Tates while Jefferson and Jerilyn learned more about the Wilsons.

Jerilyn said, "This has been the most enjoyable time. I'm glad we didn't have anything else planned."

The other three agreed, thinking, *It's so easy to forget and ignore what happened to us in the past.*

While they were all relaxed and enjoying their time together, though they had said they would decide tomorrow, they also discussed possibilities of what they might do the next day. Jefferson and Martie weren't interested in shopping for anything; that could happen anytime. They surprised their children when they told them, "We want to do something fun."

Josh and Jerilyn said, "We do too."

It was Jeff who suggested a possibility that interested all of them, and was appropriate. "How about going to the Deanna Rose Children's Farmstead?"

He explained to Martie and Josh that Overland Park had bought the land in 1971, originally designated as Community Park, then renamed in 1985 to honor Deanna Rose. She had been an Overland Park police officer under his father's oversight who was the department's first officer to die in the line of duty.

"As expected, it's geared toward children and their families, but the exhibits, activities, different animals, and demonstrations, are of interest to adults too," Jeff told them. "And there'll probably be plenty of kids to watch having fun," he added, smiling as he finished the thought.

The others could see how animated Jefferson was and realized he wanted to visit the place, and they thought it was a good choice.

~

They all enjoyed their visit to the Farmstead. Since Jerilyn was expecting, she and Josh paid special attention to the kids, especially the younger ones. Afterwards, they stopped at Fortune Wok, a Chinese restaurant on the way home, for a meal.

Jefferson laughed, saying, "Really need to prepare a meal at home before you all leave tomorrow. Use up some of the groceries I got for that purpose."

His mention of leaving brought a sad look to Martie's face. She wasn't looking forward to being separated from Jefferson again so soon. Though she knew it would happen, she wasn't ready for it, nor was he.

They had been hand in hand, and each squeezed a bit tighter as if asking, "Can we make it longer?"

Thirty-One

Before they came to Overland Park for the wedding, Jerilyn had talked to Maggie West. Maggie had made the trip with her almost two years ago to visit their friend Austen at TrailWays in Nebraska, the trip when Jerilyn met Josh. Maggie had been a church secretary and was in her church covenant group. They discussed the possibility of getting together without making any definite plans.

Now Jerilyn asked Josh, "Since we have the evening in front of us, how about I call Maggie, see if they're free, maybe go by to visit?"

All the time Jerilyn was talking to her husband, she had her eye on her dad and Martie, rightly guessing they would like some time to be together with no one else around.

She had covertly directed Josh's attention to their parents, so he agreed with her suggestion. "Sounds good. Did you say they have kids?"

"Yes, a boy and a girl."

When she called her friend, Maggie told her, "Oh, please come. We'll be glad to see you."

≈

"Okay, see you soon."

"See you later, Dad. See you later, Mom," Josh and Jerilyn waved as they went out the front door. They couldn't miss the pleased looks on their parents' faces.

~

"What do you think about that?" Jefferson asked Martie.

"What do you think?"

"Jerilyn probably does want to visit her friend. But I think she was also using it as a reason to leave us alone—to be together a bit longer."

They were at the table, finishing up cups of coffee and pieces of pecan pie. Jefferson stood, took Martie's hand, and asked, "How about going to the couch where we can sit closer together?"

She gladly assented, but before they headed for the couch, he wrapped his arms around her, and hers went around him in a warm hug. They smiled then moved into a kiss, tentative at first, then deepening into one unlike any they had shared before. With their arms still around each other, they stood, heads together, then moved to the couch, sitting close together, hands clasped.

No words for a time, both of them dazed at what the kiss had become. It brought to the forefront questions that had been in their minds. *What are we going to do about us? What's going to happen in the end? I want to be with you for always.*

Jefferson was somewhat surprised when it was Martie who was first to voice her feelings. "We have said 'I love you', and there is no longer a question. I do love you and I don't want to continue to be separated. No, I have no answer to how that can be changed.

"When will I even see you again after we leave tomorrow?"

For the time, Jefferson said nothing, just pulled her closer with his arms around her, taken aback at her words.

"I feel the same. But for now, don't think we can change what is planned for tomorrow. We can begin planning for the time after that, and I don't think we want to just move in together, wherever we are?"

Martie actually laughed and told him, "No. Besides, that wouldn't be a good example for our kids."

Jefferson said, "I can't think of any events coming up that you and I could be/would be expected to be at the same place."

"Except our grandchild," Martie reminded him.

"Yes. Though that's still months away. At least we know it will be in Nebraska."

Martie asked, "Do you want to plan a trip to Nebraska before that?"

"If I do, would I stay with you?" he asked.

"Ah, a poet," from Martie.

"Huh?"

"Never mind," she said. "Yes, stay with me. Just not sure what Josh and Jerilyn might think. But, if you remember, she stayed with him when she came for Austen's wedding, then again when she came to visit before their marriage."

"Ah, yes," Jeff remembered. "Would we tell them ahead of time? Or would I just show up?"

He had continued to hold her hand and brought it to his lips for a kiss.

Adding to his thoughts, he said, "I heard there are special activities at TrailWays on July Fourth. Maybe I could come for that?"

Martie said, "That's less than a week, you know."

"Oh yeah."

She squeezed his hand, leaned against him, then told him, "I feel more content after talking about the possibles, and knowing you feel the same as I do.

"When I get home, I'll check the calendar, see what's coming up; you can do the same. Since I've just been here, let's figure out a time you can come to me?"

Jefferson leaned over to give her a kiss. "Sounds good. How long do you want me to stay?"

Almost seriously, Martie told him, "Forever."

At that, they heard the kids' car drive up and separated slightly. Martie kissed him, then continued, "I'll call you after we've had a chance to check dates."

~

When Jerilyn and Josh came in, they couldn't tell from their demeanor if it had been a good time or otherwise for their parents, which was fine with Jeff and Martie. They weren't ready for their kids to know how strongly they felt about each other.

Jeff asked the two, "So how was your visit?"

"It was good," Jerilyn told him. "We talked a lot about the trip Maggie and I took to TrailWays. Neither of us had ever driven farther than fifty or sixty miles, had no idea how tiring a long trip can be.

"Her husband, Terry, said they have discussed the possibility of driving there for a vacation next year. As young as they are, the kids are even excited about the idea. They want to ride in a wagon, see Chimney Rock."

"How old are they?" Martie asked.

Jerilyn told her, "Jonah's eight, Harper is four. They sure are cute." Mentioning the kids, she had placed her hands on her stomach as if thinking about her expected child. Josh wrapped his arms around her, then kissed her, both of them smiling as if they were already proud parents.

Jefferson and Martie hugged too, their coming grandchild on their minds.

~

A little more conversation, then Josh asked, "What did you two do this afternoon, anything exciting?"

Not wanting to say too much that might give away their future plans, Jeff told him, "Oh, we talked about when we all might be together again, if it might be before Baby arrives," knowing that if he made the first trip, they would all be together.

Looking at their kids, Martie and Jefferson noted a look of disappointment. *What might they have expected?*

Jeff interrupted the contemplating to say, "It's been awhile since we ate. Is anybody hungry? How would you feel about ordering pizza?"

They all agreed pizza would be good, then, while they awaited its delivery, Jerilyn asked about the next day. "Dad, were you thinking about cooking breakfast tomorrow? If not, maybe we could go to First Watch, perhaps mid-morning, which could take care of lunch too. That would give us time to come back here, get everything ready for our leaving."

At those words, Jefferson and Martie reached for the other's hand, needing that connection as they deliberated being separated again.

~

While they enjoyed the pizza, Jeff asked the expectant parents if they had yet settled on names for their child. When they told him, "No," he suggested the four of them could think of some names, write them on pieces of paper, and put them in a hat. "Then you could draw out one for a boy and one for a girl."

They all laughed at the idea, but Jerilyn said, "No, don't think we'll do that."

～

They all enjoyed the time at First Watch. There was much conversation about the wedding on Saturday. Josh said, "Probably won't be any more weddings any time soon."

He missed the looks between his mother and Jerilyn's father. Josh knew they cared for each other but had no idea their feelings were that strong—that they might actually want to be married—so they could always be together.

Returning to Jeff's home, there was only time to gather all their things and double check to be sure nothing was missed. Since they had rented a car for the weekend, they would need to head for the airport sooner to have time to return it.

Josh told Jeff it had been good to see him again, thanked him for the hospitality, then picked up some of the bags to carry to the car while Jerilyn and Martie made their goodbyes.

"It's been so wonderful to be with you, Dad," Jerilyn told him with a smile. "I'm glad we had this extra time together." There was a hug and a bit of weeping, always some sadness at partings.

Martie had lingered out of sight, not wanting her son and daughter-in-law to see her tears and hoping she could repress them before she left the house. Jerilyn was now with Josh and called to her mother-in-law, "Martie, we'll wait for you at the car."

"Okay, be right out."

She was standing beside Jefferson when she made that statement, then leaned into him when his arms went around her.

"Wish I didn't have to go," she told him. "I've been so happy being here with you, so hope you can come to me soon. I love you."

There were tears in his eyes, too, as he kissed her and told her, "I love you."

Arm in arm, they went to the door, separating just before reaching it. There was one more kiss and he stayed standing at the open door. She reached the car. Josh had opened the door and helped her into the back seat.

"You okay, Mom?"

"I will be," keeping her head down, hoping he wouldn't notice the evidence of tears.

Thirty-Two

Martie thought she was successful in masking the sadness she felt at leaving Jefferson, but Jerilyn had missed none of it. Perhaps she was remembering the times not that long ago when she had the same feelings, wondering if there would ever be a time that she and Josh wouldn't be separated.

For the time being, she would say nothing to her mother-in-law, or even to Josh. What would she say anyway? What could she say in a positive way? She had watched her father and Martie when they were together and had seen enough to consider they might want to be married to each other. Now, she could sense it was in their minds. Glancing at Martie, she noticed that her eyes were closed, but there was still that hint of sadness.

By the time they were in line for boarding at the airport, Martie had regained much of her normal composure except for that despondent feeling that could be naturally expected.

The three talked about what a wonderful weekend it had been from their arrival—the wedding and all it entailed, then the extra time at Jeff's. Martie didn't add much, but Jerilyn noticed her sweet smile.

I would so much like to know what she's thinking. And how is Dad since we drove away?

~

Jeff could hardly watch as the car left, driving toward the airport. He had enjoyed the time with all of them, but especially Martie. He would never have imagined when he first met her, not quite a year ago, that she would have come to mean so much to him.

Does Jerilyn know? If so, what does she think about it? And what might Josh think? I guess they will know when—if—I go visit her and stay at her house. Now, what am I going to do with the rest of the day? The rest of the week?

In answer to the first part of the question, Jeff stepped into the room that had been Martie's. He looked around, wondering what changes should be made to make it more special, to fit her. He sat on the daybed as thoughts overcame him.

Ah, Joyce, you were so perfect for me, and I still miss you as I know Martie misses her Andrew. No one for either of us since we lost you. Now, she and I seem to fit together in the same way—unexpected for both of us. Was it God's leading? Is it sacrilegious to believe that?

Jeff checked the time as he left the room. It would be awhile before Martie was home and he could call, hear her voice again. For now, with nothing needing to be done, he started a letter, wanting to put his feelings into words.

Dear Martie,

You have been gone only minutes, but I can almost feel each mile that takes you farther away. First in the car, then the plane.

I want there to be a time we won't have to face that separation. I believe you feel the same way. When I come to you (when can that be?) I would like—love—to start plans for that possibility.

Love,

Jefferson

Martie was glad she was sitting separately from the kids on the plane. Probably didn't make much sense, but she felt that without their close presence, she could think more about Jefferson and their possible future together without wondering what they might think.

First thing to consider was when that man might come to visit and what they might do with their time. *Maybe he could come for my birthday. Would be special to have him with me. Can't think of anything unusual happening in town that might be of interest.*

While Martie was contemplating what-ifs, Jerilyn said something to Josh that startled him. "I think our parents want to get married." She had meant to wait longer before voicing her thoughts on the subject to her husband, but it seemed like a good time.

At that statement, Josh turned to look at his mother, who was a couple of rows behind them. "I have noticed they seem to like being together. What makes you think they want to get married?"

"Just watching them, mostly. Hard to explain, but when they've been together, then their separations, I can almost feel their distress, knowing they will be so far apart. Makes me remember how I felt when you and I weren't together. I know you've seen it, too, maybe just didn't want to accept it."

"You're right. Kind of different thinking about your mother wanting to marry someone, especially your father-in-law." The last said with a grin on his face, indicating maybe it wasn't such a bad postulation. Besides, he had thought about it and even considered that possibility. Since neither had said anything, it hadn't occurred to him that Jerilyn might feel the same.

Martie had relaxed from her musing when she looked to where Josh and Jerilyn were sitting two rows ahead. They were facing each other, and she could see they were smiling, then there was a kiss. *Wonder what that's about. Seems special.* Her eyes were still on them when they looked back at her, still smiling. Now she really had questions.

For the rest of the flight, Josh and Jerilyn discussed a possible marriage of their parents. Josh wondered, "Should I mention any of this to Nancy?"

"I think she probably already has an idea," his wife told him.

That surprised Josh. "What makes you think that?"

"She has seen the same things we have—maybe not the kisses. But remember, she wondered about the likelihood and we told her we had seen it."

"Oh yeah. What about your brothers?"

"The same. Don't believe they have seen any kisses either," Jerilyn told him. "The biggest question for me is, 'Where will they live'?"

That was a brand new thought for Josh. "Hadn't even considered that. Maybe they'll decide to live in Nebraska half the time, and in Kansas the other half."

"Maybe."

"Are we going to ask Mom?" Josh wondered.

"No."

"Why not?"

"We need to let her tell us," Jerilyn told him. "She may wonder how much we know, but I think she hopes we don't really have a clue. I won't say anything to Dad, either."

"Sort of like a secret that's not a secret," Josh said.

"Exactly," Jerilyn agreed, leaning over to give him a kiss.

~

They were in Scottsbluff at the airport, waiting at the carousel for their luggage. Josh and Jerilyn were hand in hand, glad to be almost home, though they had enjoyed the time in Overland Park. Martie was standing nearby wearing a lost, confused look.

Thinking about their conversation on the plane about their parents, Jerilyn went to her mother-in-law and hugged her.

"Late as it is, how about you spend the night with us? We can order something from Eddie's for a meal when we get home. One of us will take you home in the morning."

It was a spur-of-the-moment thought. Jerilyn had said nothing to her husband before speaking to his mother. She could tell it was unexpected and neither knew what Martie's response might be.

She was obviously surprised at the invitation, but Martie shocked them both when she said, "Oh, that will be so nice, thank you!"

Her conduct immediately changed, and she was smiling when she spotted her suitcases.

Since she had been separated from Josh and Jerilyn on the plane, Martie had been unable to voice her feelings about the few days at Jeff's. So as soon as they were settled in the car, she said, "The time in Overland Park sure went by fast; guess it's because there was so much activity."

Josh and Jerilyn couldn't help smiling, thinking about the times their parents were together.

"Yes," Jerilyn said. "Seems like there's never enough time for everything. Maybe I'm just sensing that more since I'm getting older."

Josh agreed, saying, "I'm older than you, so time is really flying by." He had reached for his wife's hand and kissed it before releasing it.

Martie watched them, grateful for them both and the love they had for each other—the kind she had with Andrew and she believed would be with Jefferson—a lasting one.

Now she asked Jerilyn, "Have you been in touch with your dad since we're back in Nebraska?"

"I haven't. How about you?"

"Not yet," Martie told her. "I'll call when we get to your house."

~

Jefferson answered with, "I hoped you would call. You must be home."

"Actually, I'm at Josh's. He and Jerilyn invited me to spend the night. We've ordered supper from Eddie's; they'll take me home tomorrow."

"That's good. Is there a reason?" Jefferson wondered. Martie told him, "Mostly just being tired, I guess. I'm glad for it. I was dreading going home, being by myself."

Jefferson agreed, "I can sure understand that. I'm here alone again. Guess that means you haven't had a chance to check your calendar for a time I might visit?"

"I haven't," Martie told him, "but I have an idea. My birthday is July twenty-third. Would be good to have you here for that."

"I'll put it on my calendar. Maybe we can talk about it tomorrow? I'm thinking I might drive."

"We can both think about it. Now, supper's here, so guess I need to say bye. Love you."

"Love you too. Bye."

~

Jerilyn had done her best to be discreet and give her mother-in-law complete privacy. Despite that, she did hear the "love you."

Thirty-Three

While they were eating, Josh could see there was something on his wife's mind. *What happened since we got home?*

Now he asked his mom, "How's Jeff?"

Martie flashed her son a look, wondering about his question. After a moment, considering all they had talked about, she chose to tell them both.

"He's sad being home alone."

"Any ideas about when you will see him again?"

She gazed at her son, turned her attention to Jerilyn, and said, "He may come for my birthday." Knowing Jerilyn probably didn't know when that was, Martie told her, "It's July twenty-third."

"Not long," Jerilyn noted.

Deciding they might as well know everything, Martie told them, "He said he might drive." She paused. "He'll stay with me."

Her son and daughter-in-law turned their attention to each other, remembering their conversation on the plane. They stood, walked to where Martie was sitting, took her hands to help her stand, wrapped their arms around her for a group hug, then both said, "Okay, good."

Martie was astonished, having no idea of all the two had observed then surmised after watching their parents together.

Josh and Jerilyn began clearing the table when he asked, "Did we order any dessert?"

"No," Jerilyn told him, "but there are brownies in the freezer. We can warm some up in the microwave."

Martie was still wondering, *What was that hug about? What did the words mean?* when she said, "Brownies—sounds good. Then I definitely need to head for bed."

Her son asked, "What time do you want to go home tomorrow, after breakfast or after lunch?"

"How about after breakfast? Maybe leave here about nine-thirty?"

"Sounds perfect. No one will need to rush. What will you do the rest of the day?"

"Unpack, check the flower beds, maybe see if I need groceries," his mother told him.

"Will you call Jeff again?" Josh asked.

Martie was surprised at the question, thinking again about the earlier words and the hug, but told him, "Probably."

≈

Jerilyn let Josh take his mother home. She planned to call her dad; and thinking of the 'love you' she had heard from Martie, wanted to be alone when she did so. At the same time, she wondered if the two had talked since then.

She hadn't told her husband about the overheard words. And she might not say anything to her dad. Maybe he would mention them himself.

When she started the call she hoped Jeff would be free and could answer. It was easy to forget there was an hour difference in time, and he could be busy.

"Hello, Jerilyn."

"Hi, Dad. Glad you're home. Thought you might be occupied with some activity and I would have to leave a message."

"Not much going on here," he told her. "There seems to always be something happening at OPHS, not sure I'll join them.

"How about you? Will you and Josh be busy at TrailWays on the Fourth? Maybe Martie, too? If you all hadn't just been here, maybe I would join you."

"Josh and I will be there to help however we can. Not sure about Martie. She told us you're coming for her birthday."

That surprised Jeff. "Yes, we talked about it when we were deciding on a time for me to visit—maybe an excuse to visit. It's still quite awhile before Baby arrives."

His daughter told him, "You do know we would be glad to see you any time."

No answer from Jeff.

After a short pause, she continued, "But I know you want to be with Martie, as she wants to be with you.

"Dad?"

"You're right," he finally responded.

Jerilyn admitted to him, "I heard her 'love you' at the end of her call to you.

"And I love you too. Josh and I have been with you two enough the past several days that we couldn't miss seeing your feelings for each other.

"And we certainly experienced times of separations when we couldn't be together, like you and Martie."

"Yes."

"Anyway," his daughter continued, "wanted you to know we love our parents and hope for happiness for you."

Jeff said, "Guess you can tell I'm surprised. Don't know why Martie and I haven't realized how much all of you have witnessed.

"Yes, I love her too, and just like you and Josh, we're not sure how or when things might change. We do want to be together."

"I haven't told Josh about hearing the 'love you'," Jerilyn said. "But he's seen the same things I have."

"And you know the rest of the kids—Jack and Jon and Nancy aren't blind either."

Jeff asked, "So we don't have to be sneaky?"

Laughing, Jerilyn said, "No."

"Josh took Martie home. You knew she spent the night here?"

"Yes."

"He'll probably be back soon. Guess it's okay to tell him our parents are in love with each other?"

Jeff said, "That sounds different … parents in love with each other." Then laughing, added, "Parents should be in love with each other. Knowing you know will make it easier for us, no tiptoeing around."

His daughter told him, "I'm so glad we were able to talk about this. Look forward to seeing you end of July. Love you. Bye."

"And I love you. Bye."

❧

While Jerilyn was talking to her dad, Josh was talking to his mom. Her house wasn't that far from her son's, so it took little time to get there.

He carried her luggage in and checked around to make sure all was well since Martie had been away several days. Josh hadn't intended to stay, but his question earlier about whether she would call Jeff again remained in his mother's mind.

Now she asked him, "Can you stay awhile?"

Wondering why since they had been together the past few days, he said, "Sure. Is there a reason?"

"You could say so … Would you like coffee or …"

"No coffee. Water would be good."

Martie fixed glasses of ice water for both of them and set them on the table. When they were seated, without preface, she told her son, "I love Jefferson Tate," then waited for a response from him.

"Yeah, Mom. I know."

No one could have missed the surprised look on her face.

"How do you know?"

Josh told her, "We've watched you two at all the weddings. There's no question there was something charismatic between you when you first met. Probably neither one of you expected there would be any-thing more.

"Since then, there's no question those feelings between you and Jeff— Jefferson— have grown. We've all seen how happy you are being together, then such a sadness when you have to separate."

Josh watched the different emotions that flashed across his mother's face as he continued, "But the fact is, when we were all together at Jeff's house, Jerilyn and I became so much more cogni-zant of how much you care for—love each other.

"Maybe it's because the circumstances so closely resemble our courtship."

"But there's still Nancy and Jerilyn's brothers. What might they think?" Martie asked.

"Mom, none of us is blind. We've all seen it and accepted it. Maybe we've just been waiting for you to tell us before saying any-thing about it. We all want you both to be happy, okay?"

Martie leaned over toward him, resting her head against her son's.

"Yes, okay, but there are still questions and decisions for Jefferson and me."

Josh assured her, "Maybe it will be easier, simpler, since you're aware that all your kids know about your love."

~

Josh had barely backed out of her driveway when Martie called Jefferson. She could hardly wait to tell him about all she and her son had discussed.

Jeff answered, "Martie! Didn't expect to hear from you yet. Just finished a long call with Jerilyn."

He was anxious to tell her about his visit with his daughter, but Martie had much to relate. He let her talk with no interruptions as she shared all that was on her mind after her visit with Josh. There was no question that she had been surprised, and he couldn't miss the happiness, and some surprise, as she conveyed the news to him.

When she paused briefly, she asked, "What do you think of all that?"

"Sounds familiar," Jefferson told her.

"What do you mean?" Martie wanted to know.

"I just had a similar conversation with Jerilyn. Guess we haven't been as guarded as we thought."

"Yes," Martie agreed. "From what Josh said, sounds like all our kids know our feelings."

"And are okay with it," Jeff pointed out. "Maybe when I'm there, we can talk about, even begin making plans, for us to be together."

"Lots to think about," Martie said.

"That's for sure. But at least we can be open about it, maybe even ask for advice."

"Hadn't considered that," Martie told him. "Advice from one's kids about a possible marriage."

Thirty-Four

All three Wilsons, Josh, Jerilyn, and Martie were at Trail-Ways for the Fourth. They were there to celebrate the special day and to help if necessary. Surrounding neighbors and people from town were there. Red, white, and blue decorations were hung everywhere, including the mules and horses. A business in town catered the food. There were games, horseback riding, maybe a trek, a band was there providing patriotic music all day.

Josh went to find Mark to learn if there might be something he needed help with. Martie was with Kate Pearson while Jerilyn and Austen were walking around checking to be sure all was going smoothly. Morgan was with them, being pushed in a stroller.

Austen said, "Next year, she'll probably be with Mark too. No question of their love for each other. I'm sure you've noticed David is already doing a lot, as always, with Mark."

Jerilyn noticed tears in her friend's eyes. "In case you're wondering about the tears," Austen said, "they're happy, wondrous tears. I'm still so overwhelmed with my love for Mark, and his for me. I could never have dreamed how my life was going to be when I quit my job and drove to Chimney Rock."

Jerilyn moved to Austen, and wrapped her arms around her friend. "And because of that, I'm here too with my love."

They hugged again, laughed, and together, said, "Thank you, God."

~

Kate Pearson had no specific duties for the day, but as she and Martie strolled around, she was almost automatically making sure everyone had all they needed. Austen had glanced their way several times and told Jerilyn, "Martie sure has a blissful aura about her. Is there a reason?"

"Actually, yes," Jerilyn told her. "She and my dad are in love."

"Ah. I've observed how they seem to like being together. So, what's going to happen with that?" Austen asked.

"There's no doubt they want that together to be forever," Jerilyn said. "Just not sure when/if it can happen.

"Dad's coming for her birthday. He may drive and will stay with her."

"When's her birthday?"

"The twenty-third."

"Not long."

"No."

~

Martie and Kate were enjoying the opportunity to just visit and catch up on what was happening in their lives. Martie hadn't noticed, but occasionally, Kate would glance at her with a quizzical look, trying to interpret what was different about her.

"How were your extra days in Overland Park after the wedding?" she asked Martie. "Did you do anything special?"

She was facing Martie when she asked the question, so couldn't miss her sweet smile. *What does that mean? Will she give me an answer?*

"Mat—, er, Martie."

"Oh, I'm sorry."

"Looks like something is on your mind … Something good?"

"Yes. Jefferson had bought groceries in anticipation of preparing meals for more people," Martie said. "But we ended up eating out. Some of the places were new to me."

Kate was disappointed. She had been sure something more than new eating places had produced that happy expression.

Martie knew her answer was not what Kate had hoped to hear, so she added, "And Jefferson and I have admitted our love to each other."

Kate's mouth opened in a stunned, "Oh! I hadn't expected that, but I can't say I'm surprised. I watched you two at Nancy's wedding.

"Any plans for your future?"

"Not yet. So much to consider. He's coming for my birthday, will stay a few days. Maybe after that. Though I remember when Jerilyn came to visit Josh after they were engaged. They expected to make plans for their wedding, but when she went home, very little had been decided."

"Will there be a wedding for you and Jefferson?"

Martie said nothing for a while, then, only, "Hopefully," not ready to add more. Everything was still so new.

Kate had hoped to ask if Martie's and Jefferson's kids knew about the feelings their parents had for each other. But she could tell Martie had said all she was going to—at least for now.

～

As it always was, it had been a day enjoyed by all the Wilsons, but tiring, too, especially for Jerilyn. It was mid-afternoon when she said, "It's been a wonderful day, and I don't want to miss the fireworks, but I'm pooped, need a nap."

Josh suggested, "How about I take you home for a couple of hours, then come back? There's nothing I'm needed for here," then pulled her into his arms.

Jerilyn hugged him tightly and said, "That would be so good. Have I told you today that I love you?"

"Don't remember, but I'm always glad to hear it.

"I'll find Mom, let her know we're leaving for a while, see what she might want to do."

"I could stand a nap too," she told him. "Besides, I want to call Jefferson, see what he's done today."

They dropped Martie off and Josh told her, "I'll call when we're leaving the house to pick you up."

~

Jeff was glad to hear from Martie and answered with, "Hello, Love. Happy Independence Day. Are you celebrating?"

"And love to you," Martie said. "Yes. Have spent much of the day at TrailWays, think you and I talked about that. We'll go back for the fireworks. We left because Jerilyn needed a nap and I needed to call you.

"Have you celebrated in any way?"

"Not yet, just hanging around the house," Jefferson told her. "Will go to Corporate Woods for the fireworks later. Both boys are on duty but will be there too.

"They had to cancel one year because of flooding of a nearby creek, but except for that, it's an annual event, promoted as a Star

Spangled Spectacular. There are concerts from several bands, food trucks, and of course the fireworks.

"Maybe you and I can celebrate together next year."

"Yes," Martie said. "I hope so. Any special plans for the rest of the week?"

"No, how about you?"

She told him, "I don't either. Just looking forward to when you're here and considering what we might do."

"Yeah, me too. I'm so glad we got to visit. Love you."

"And I love you."

There were "byes" together.

Though they were both looking forward to the fireworks later, both Jefferson and Martie felt a little desolate after their visit. They would be together for her birthday, but that was almost three weeks away.

~

The days after the Fourth and before Martie's birthday seemed to be twice as long as they should be—forty-eight hours, instead of twenty-four. Martie and Jefferson talked nearly every day, and there were emails too. Much of their conversations were about what they would do when he was in Plattsford. There had been no specific date mentioned for his arrival. It was as if the twenty-third was the day.

Then, shortly after one of their phone visits, Jefferson thought, *Why don't I go early? Being there for her birthday is most important, but we can enjoy time together before.*

He immediately sent an email to Martie with those thoughts, then texted his son-in-law to learn his thoughts about a special gift for her.

Thirty-Five

Josh wondered who was texting him. Anyone who wanted to get in touch with him just called. When he saw it was from his father-in-law, he wondered even more, *Why would Jeff text me instead of Jerilyn?*

Jeff's text read, "*Hi, Josh. Think you know I will be in Plattsford to help celebrate your mom's birthday. I want to get her something special. Hope you might have some ideas. Thanks, Jeff.*"

Josh thought, *This is a better question for my sister. I'll check with her. Jerilyn may have ideas too.*

Meantime, he sent a text to Jeff. "*Yeah, knew you were coming for Mom's birthday. I'll consider what she might like. Going to ask Nancy and Jerilyn, too, for ideas.*"

They had just finished breakfast, but still at the table when Josh received the text. Noticing the look of puzzlement on her husband's face, she asked, "So what is it? Is there a problem?"

"Maybe. It's from your dad."

Now she wore that same confused look. "Dad? What about?"

Josh told her about Jeff wanting suggestions for a gift for Martie. "I can't think of anything right off. How about you?"

"No, maybe Nancy?"

"Yeah, I plan to check with her." Then he asked, "What might you like for a special gift?"

They were both standing, and he had walked to her, wrapped his arms around her before he asked the question. Now he told her, "You are a special gift for me."

"And you are to me," followed by a kiss.

~

At first, Nancy had no ideas either, then she texted, "How about a cat?"

Holding up his phone, Josh told Jerilyn, "It's from Nancy. She wonders about a cat."

Surprised at the suggestion, Jerilyn asked, "A cat?"

"Yeah, not really a bad idea. We had cats on the ranch, but none since moving into town. And I know Mom loves cats. She used to talk about getting one, but it never happened.

"What might your dad think?"

"No idea."

Josh asked, "Did you have cats when you were growing up?"

"We did," Jerilyn answered. "Don't remember Dad paying much attention to them."

"Would you like to have one now?"

"Why don't we concentrate on choosing one for your mom? Maybe think about it after Baby is born."

"Sounds good," Josh said. "I'll let Nancy know we agree with her, then text your dad. Or do you just want to call him?"

"Yes, but before I do, is there a specific breed we need to consider?"

"I don't know. She seemed to like the ones with long, fluffy hair, whatever breed that might be."

"Maybe Nancy knows. I'll call Dad anyway, let him know our suggestions."

~

It was the end of the day when Jerilyn made the call. Jeff asked, "Did Josh tell you I need gift suggestions for your mother-in-law?"

"He did. We checked with Nancy too."

"So, do you have any ideas?" he wanted to know.

"We do; you may think it's strange."

Jefferson responded, "Ah, sounds interesting, what are they?"

"Only one," his daughter told him.

"That should make it easy."

"Well, maybe," Jerilyn said. "Both Josh and Nancy think their mom would like a cat."

No comment from Jeff.

"Dad?"

Finally, he said, "A cat … Well, that's certainly different. Any special kind?"

"Josh said she used to like the fluffy ones."

"Whatever that means."

Jerilyn told him, "I think you can figure it out. And, of course, you will have to get everything needed to make it comfortable."

"That will take some thought," her dad said. "But I think I like the idea."

~

Jon and Linda had invited his dad, as well as Jack and Jayden, for supper the next evening. They enjoyed the meal, and as they were all cleaning up, Jeff told them about the idea for Martie's birthday gift.

Both Jayden and Linda liked the idea and wondered if he planned "to get the cat here?"

"I guess," Jeff answered. "What do you think?"

After discussion among all of the young people, they concluded it could work, but said, "You might want to take it for a couple of short rides in your SUV before heading out for western Nebraska."

~

Jeff still planned to go to Martie's before her birthday. That meant he didn't have much time to shop for a cat and all the accouterments to take care of it, as well as taking it for some rides.

The next day, he decided to visit a couple of pet stores. *I don't have any recent experience with cats. Maybe I'll find one that likes me.*

He walked around at the first one, noting the different kinds of cats, trying to determine their personalities. Most were cute, but it was obvious they weren't happy being in cages. Jeff felt they were begging to be released.

Then he visited one where the enclosures were roomier and even opened onto a play area enclosed with a low fence. All the kittens were bouncing around in a lively manner and ran toward any customers.

Jeff had his eye on the fluffy ones, enjoying their exuberance, when he noticed a specific cute, inquisitive one. It cocked its head to the side as if to get a closer look at him. It was a calico. He vaguely remembered Joyce having one so many years ago. Might Martie like one too?

People who were seriously looking for pets were allowed to pick up and pet the animals. Jeff thought, *I might as well see how friendly this cutie is.* The kitten seemed to want to cuddle and meowed as if saying, *take me.*

That's all he needed to choose it as the special gift for Martie. He let the clerk know, then, with her help, selected everything else on his list.

When he got home with the cat, Jeff thought, *Kitty survived that trip okay. When shall I take her for the next one? Need to make sure her space in the house is secure. Don't want her to escape.*

After getting Kitty settled, another topic invaded Jeff's mind. *I think the boys know I'm in love with Martie. Should I tell them I'm going to propose? If I do, it should be in person. Maybe we can meet at Cinzetti's for a meal. I could tell them there.*

Since he planned to head to Plattsford in a couple of days, he needed to ask now. He sent texts to his sons asking, *"What's your schedule? Would like to take you out to eat before my trip—Jayden and Linda, too. I found a kitten for Martie."*

Jon and Jack talked it over with their wives, then Jack called his dad.

"All four of us are available tomorrow, but we'd like to see the cat. So, how about us ordering pizza to be delivered to your house and we all come there?"

"Sounds good. Evening?"

"Yes, see you then."

~

They all enjoyed the pizza as well as the pecan pie Jayden had brought from the store. Slices of it were in front of each of them when Jeff stood, a serious look on his face.

He reached to pat the shoulders of his sons, then said, "This has been a great time. Thank you all. As you know, I'll be driving to Nebraska in a couple of days to visit Martie. Of course, I'll see your sister, too.

"Your mother and I loved each other so much. I could hardly bear it when she died." He paused when tears filled his eyes, then continued, "Didn't expect there would ever be anyone else for me, that there might be a time I would love again."

There were more tears, from him and his sons. They stood and wrapped their arms around his shoulders.

"Sorry," he said. "Anyway, I believe you know I'm in love with Martie, and she loves me. We want to be together, though no idea yet where that will be.

"I plan to visit with her kids, Josh and Nancy, to get their permission, then I'm going to propose. I wanted you all to know that."

Jeff was surprised when his sons and daughters-in-law gathered around him for a group hug.

Jack told him, "Yes, we knew you loved each other, and we have been around Martie enough to care for her too. You will be in our prayers as you proceed with the plans for your future."

Thirty-Six

Josh and Jerilyn had told Jeff that Martie's birthday dinner would be at their house. He would be arriving before that day, so asked their permission to leave Kitty and everything to take care of her at their house.

When Jeff dropped the cat off, he told Josh, "I would like to meet with you and Nancy when we're all here. Maybe you can mention it to her? I hope Jerilyn and Mitchell can occupy your mom's attention at the same time."

At first, his son-in-law wondered why, but soon figured out the reason and smiled when he shared with his wife, telling her, "You and Mitch may have to divert mom's attention for a while."

Jefferson left for Martie's as soon as Kitty was settled in the space Jerilyn and Josh had prepared for her. It was late in the day, and Martie didn't know whether or not to be worried about him. She had received texts all through the day since he left OP very early in the morning.

Martie checked the last one. He had stopped for gas and mentioned seeing a sign indicating *80 miles to Chimney Rock*. Mileage to Plattsford should be less. If there had been no trouble, Jefferson should be here.

Expecting he would be tired, Martie had prepared a meal including the meatloaf he had liked. Food could be warmed up but would taste so much better without that need.

Just as she considered sending a text to him, Jefferson's car pulled into her driveway. With a smile, she rushed to the front door, opened it, and was at the car door almost before he stopped. He turned off the engine and stepped out into Martie's arms. They hugged, then with his arms around her, Jefferson lifted her up for a kiss.

"I'm so glad you're here," she told him. "I was getting worried."

"I'm glad I'm here too. Sorry you were worried."

One more kiss, then he grabbed his luggage, locked the SUV, and they headed for the house where Martie held the door open for him. Still holding the bags, he said, "Ah, something smells good."

"I thought you might be hungry when you got here, and probably worn out. I tried to gauge when you would arrive so we can have a meal here, no need to get back in the car and drive even more."

Martie led Jefferson to the room which would be his for however long he stayed. "Since supper's ready, why don't you just set your suitcases down? You can unpack after."

"Sounds good. I do need to wash up a bit before we eat."

"Okay. I'll see you in the kitchen."

He took her hand, kissed her, and said, "Soon."

~

By the time they finished the meal, it was apparent Jefferson was at the end of his energy. Martie said, "Much as I would like more time with you, I think you need to get in bed."

"I should help you clean up."

"If you didn't look so tired, I would let you," she told him. "Let me walk you to your room. We have a new day tomorrow to look forward to."

When they reached his room, she told him, "I'm so glad you're here."

"So am I."

There was a special kiss as they stood with arms around each other. "Do you want me to wake you in the morning?" Martie asked.

"Yes, knock on my door as soon as you're up. I love you."

"And I love you."

Reluctantly separating, Jefferson went into his room and waved at Martie before closing the door. Martie was tired, too, after her concern for Jefferson during the day, but she took time to clean the kitchen before heading to bed herself.

~

Jeff woke slowly, forgetting for a while he was in a bed in Martie's home. They had agreed that she would knock on his door when she was up. Seemed that despite how tired he was at the end of the day before, his body was still adjusted to the time in Overland Park—an hour ahead of Plattsford.

Unexpectedly, Martie woke up earlier than usual. Was it because of the special man sleeping in another room? Then she remembered the hour's difference in time. *Might he be awake already?*

Jeff was surprised to hear the knock but told Martie, "I'm awake."

She said, "Good. I'll get dressed, then meet you in the kitchen."

~

They reached the kitchen at the same time and walked into each other's arms, kissed, and said, "Good morning!"

They stood, smiling at each other for a while, then Martie asked, "Are you hungry?"

Jefferson grinned, and said, "Yes, I am," but didn't complete what he was thinking, *"Hungry for you."* How had that come to be?

Jeff usually had cereal for breakfast. Martie made scrambled eggs, toast, and bacon. Though she might have only toast and coffee most days, and she told him so.

"Ah. Something special for today. Thank you."

During breakfast, they discussed how they might spend the day. Martie reminded them both that when Jefferson was there for Nancy's wedding, they had driven through the countryside.

"Think it's going to be cooler for a summer day. What would you think about walking around the blocks nearby, meet some of my neighbors?"

Some of them knew about her special feelings for Jefferson, and Martie had in mind that if they should marry, she and Jefferson might live here.

"Sounds good to me, could use a little exercise."

When they began their walk, Martie told him, "Some of these people lived here when we moved in. What about your neighbors?"

"I've lived there so long I don't believe any of them were there when we moved in. But they have all been friendly."

They enjoyed the leisurely stroll. Both mentioned it was something they hadn't done for a while. It was a good thing, a chance to get acquainted or reacquainted with those who lived nearby.

Some knew about Martie's birthday and asked if there were any special plans to celebrate the occasion. She told them, "Jefferson hasn't experienced much of TrailWays, and I can't remember when

I have, so tomorrow afternoon, we'll take a short trek to Chimney Rock.

"We'll go to Josh and Jerilyn's in the evening. Nancy and Mitchell will be there."

~

At the end of their walk, when they entered Martie's yard, Jefferson asked, "How about giving me a tour of your flower beds?"

She agreed and also pointed out the plants and flowers she had given to Jerilyn for her garden.

"Yeah. I need to check hers, too, while I'm still here."

~

The next day, Jefferson and Martie went to Eddie's Café for brunch before they went to TrailWays. He already had a hat and had purchased boots in preparation for his trip to Nebraska. Though she didn't wear them often, Martie had boots, so as many visitors did, they were dressed in western wear for their scheduled journey.

It took little time for Jefferson to grasp why Chimney Rock was such a popular site and still astounded visitors just as it had for those families headed for Oregon in the 1840s.

Martie said, "You might think it would be humdrum to us since we live here and see it every day, but seeing it up close still inspires."

~

When they returned to Martie's, she and Jefferson both showered, then took naps to be refreshed for the birthday celebration at

Josh and Jerilyn's. Before he left his room, Jeff texted Jerilyn, *"Wondering how Kitty is. Hope she hasn't given you any trouble. Looking forward to tonight. Sure hope Martie won't be disappointed."*

Jerilyn's return text read, *"Kitty is fine. We love her. Maybe we'll keep her if Martie doesn't want her."*

On their way to the party, Jefferson noticed Martie glancing around the car as if she was looking for something. He smiled, thinking, *she's probably wondering if I have a gift for her.*

She seemed even more puzzled, and maybe disappointed, when they exited the car. *I hope she will be pleased with Kitty.*

Jerilyn and Mitch greeted Martie as soon as she entered the house, asking how her birthday had been so far, what had she and Jeff done? Jeff noticed where Josh and Nancy were, and as soon as they had greeted their mother, they and Jefferson met in the room where Kitty was.

The three hugged, already a special feeling between them. Then Jeff took one of Nancy's hands and one of Josh's.

"I'm sure you know why I wanted to meet with you. I never expected to love again after Joyce died. But from the time of our first meeting, Martie has been special to me. That first liking has grown into love, and we've expressed our love to each other. I don't know where we might settle, but I want to ask her to marry me. And it would mean so much to me to have your approval.

"If she says, 'yes,' I plan to take her to the jeweler in Scottsbluff to choose rings."

Nancy and Josh released their hands and again wrapped their

arms around Jefferson. Nancy told him, "There's no question that our mom loves you. I will be glad to have you in our family."

Josh seconded his sister's words, laughed, and said, "Boy, you're already my father-in-law. To have you as a stepfather doubles the affection."

It wasn't time to present gifts yet, so Kitty was left in the room as they exited.

Thirty-Seven

fter Martie had visited with Mitch and Jerilyn for a while, she saw that her children and Jefferson weren't in the room. When they came in, she noticed tears in Jefferson's eyes and wondered what they meant.

Jerilyn was watching, and as soon as she saw her dad, she said, "Okay, everybody, food is ready. Josh will give thanks, then you can fill your plates and find a seat at the table.

~

The kitchen had been cleaned up when the special cake from Eddie's was brought out and set beside the stacks of plates and silverware. Jerilyn arranged the number candles representing her mother-in-law's age on the cake.

"Martie, are you ready to make a wish?"

Martie said, "Yes," then, closing her eyes, made a silent wish, or maybe it was a prayer. *I hope Jefferson and I have an enjoyable time while he's here, and before he leaves, plans have begun for a life together.*

When Martie's eyes were open, Jerilyn lit the candles, and they all sang "Happy Birthday" before she blew them out.

After they enjoyed cake and coffee, the group moved into the living room to present their gifts to their mom. Nancy and Mitchell had brought a gnome to be placed in one of Martie's flower beds.

Josh and Jerilyn had given her a gift card for the nursery so she could pick out something special. Jefferson, Josh and Jerilyn, and Mitchell and Nancy had kept their eyes on her, not missing a certain puzzlement—disappointment?

Deciding it was time to eliminate that expression, Jefferson went to get Kitty. Jerilyn had fixed up a basket for her with a pillow and a pink silk ribbon tied in a bow on the handle. Martie wondered why he left, but he was gone just a short time before returning, carrying a basket and heading toward her.

Jefferson placed the basket with Kitty in her lap and told her, "I asked your kids what I might give you for a gift that would be special to you. I hope this fills that request. We have called her Kitty, but you might have a different name for her."

As soon as the basket was in Martie's lap, Kitty climbed out, meowing as if telling her, *I like you. Do you like me?*

Martie picked her up and started stroking her. "Oh, I love you so much," then turned to Jefferson and said, "And I love you so much." He leaned down so they could kiss.

Martie told them all, "Thank you for this most wonderful celebration."

She and her kids visited awhile longer, recalling past birthdays and naming some of the gifts they received. At the same time, Jefferson was taking all of Kitty's trappings and accessories to his SUV in preparation for moving to Martie's.

He and she hadn't discussed how long he would be in Nebraska. So far, it had been only a few days. *Besides celebrating her birthday, my main purpose for coming was to propose. When will I do that? What's on the schedule for tomorrow?*

He arranged Kitty's things in the backseat, only the basket was left. Martie would probably want to hold that in her lap.

When he returned to the house, Mitch told him, "Dad asked me to invite you to visit the ranch, maybe Sunday or Monday if you're still in Nebraska."

He glanced at Martie, who was nodding her head, then answered, "We'll discuss it when we're back at Martie's, then let you know if that's okay."

"Absolutely. We all look forward to showing you around."

At Martie's, Kitty was settled while she and Jefferson were enjoying a cup of tea. She told him again, "You sure surprised me with Kitty. And, yes, I'm going to keep that name for her."

"Have to admit, I would never have thought of it myself. So, you need to thank the kids too."

Changing the subject, he said, "We haven't talked about how long I'll be here. I guess at least a couple more days since we're going to the ranch. What day do you want to go?"

"How about Monday? Save Sunday for church?"

"Sounds good. So any idea how long you'd like me to stay? Don't want to wear out my welcome."

"You couldn't do that. But let's talk about that later. Is that all your questions?"

Jefferson stood and said, "Actually, no."

He came to Martie, turned her chair away from the table, then knelt in front of her.

"I talked to Josh and Nancy and got their permission to ask you to marry me. I love you and want to spend the rest of my life with you. I know you love me too. So will you marry me, Martha Elizabeth Yates Wilson?"

Tears were streaming from Martie's eyes, even while she smiled. "Oh, definitely, positively, absolutely, yes, Jefferson Lawrence Tate."

They both stood so they could wrap their arms around each other and give the kiss they both wanted. Instead of returning to the table, Martie took Jeff's hand and led him to the couch. She wanted another special kiss before anything else.

She snuggled against Jefferson and said, "Guess we have a lot to talk about."

"Yeah, but first, how about driving into Scottsbluff tomorrow to check out rings?"

In addition to making that decision, there were other big questions they needed to face, such as, where would they live? They both had a home, and maybe they would alternate spending time in each of them. Maybe no hurry to decide.

There was also the same question Josh and Jerilyn had faced, where would the wedding be? But the most important question was when?

〜

They made the trip to Scottsbluff and chose rings, which fit perfectly, so no necessity for a return trip. Lunch at Runza's, then before heading back to Plattsford, a drive by where Nancy worked, though being Saturday, it was closed.

Thinking his sons might be wondering whether he had proposed, Jeff sent texts to them after they returned to Martie's, telling them, *"Martie liked her gift. I proposed, she accepted. Dad."*

He wasn't surprised to get return texts questioning whether a wedding date had been set and asking for any other details. Jeff let them know, *"We wonder too. Might know by the time I'm back in OP."*

Martie let Josh and Nancy know she had accepted Jefferson's proposal, knowing they wouldn't be surprised, but they, too, were curious about how soon there would be a wedding.

After contacting their kids, Martie and Jefferson walked around the yard to choose the best location for the gnome she received for her birthday and also considered what might be a good use for the gift card.

With no activities planned for the rest of the day, they sat at the table with glasses of iced tea and a calendar in front of them. With all the decisions to be made, they hardly knew what to address first. With a smile, they leaned into each other for a kiss.

Both Martie and Jefferson wanted to have a date set for their wedding and chose one, even knowing other things would be involved in the decision—a month from now in Nebraska. Even that was longer than they preferred. Other concerns could be addressed when they met with Pastor Sanders midweek.

~

Meg and Dennis congratulated Jefferson and Martie on their engagement and were surprised how soon they expected to have the wedding. Jeff enjoyed his first time on a horse, riding around a few acres at the Rocking R—a different experience sharing their space with cows and their calves. Maybe it would become a regular thing.

~

After their visit with Pastor Sanders, much more was settled regarding the wedding, the date, and rehearsal. They needed to check with TrailWays regarding the reception, and decide on attendants.

When they were discussing whether or not to have attendants, both Jefferson and Martie mentioned having their children, if the children agreed. But what might the order be with three guys and only two girls? They decided the best thing was to first find out whether the kids might even be interested before spending more time on it.

Martie did want to have a special dress for the occasion and would ask her daughter and daughter-in-law to help her choose. It might mean they would need new dresses too.

For the guys, Jefferson thought he and Josh could wear the same suits they had worn for Josh and Jerilyn's wedding, and Jack and Jon could wear their uniforms.

Martie hadn't stopped thinking about attendants, and before they called the kids, she told Jefferson, "You can be with the pastor at the front, Josh will escort me, then stand beside you, sort of as best man. Jon and Jack can escort Jerilyn and Nancy to my side, Nancy as matron of honor. One of your sons could have my ring, and one of the girls would have yours. No other attendants."

When she finished her thoughts, Jefferson wrapped his arms around her and said, "I think it's perfect."

They then called the kids instead of texting, so there could be some discussion, and were pleased when they all seemed excited about the idea. For Jeff's sons and their spouses, they would need to be sure to have time off from work. Hopefully, that wouldn't be a problem.

Once that was taken care of, Jefferson reminded Martie they had been ignoring one thing. "I still have to return to Overland Park."

"And we need to decide about invitations," she added.

Thirty-Eight

When he was home, going through his clothes, deciding which ones to take to Nebraska, Jeff smiled. *If I'm going to wear this suit for my wedding, I need to get it cleaned.* Except for the suit, when he got back to Plattsford, he left most of the clothes in the suitcases, waiting until after the wedding to move them to closets and bureau drawers.

Since he was going to ask the old cops to keep an eye on his house, he planned a last get-together—pizza ordered in instead of having a cookout. He was surprised that they brought a wedding gift—a throw. One of them told him, "We figured you probably don't need anything, but you can think of us when you wrap yourselves in it."

∿

Before he left to return to Overland Park, Jefferson and Martie made a list for invitations. Jerilyn and Nancy helped her address them, though for some who received them, it might seem more like an announcement since it was such a short time before that special day.

In fact, that was true of Martie's brother Brent and his family, who lived in Lincoln. Though they didn't see each other often, they kept in close touch. Martie had mentioned Jefferson to them and how they met but hadn't conveyed how important he was to her. The family hadn't gone to Nancy's wedding just a few months before, but he and Mary would make sure to attend the one of his sister.

~

Jeff's sons and their wives drove in the day before rehearsal. Mark and Austen Thomas had reserved spots at TrailWays for them. They all learned that Mitchell Robbins's cousin, Nate Williams, and his fiancée, Carly Black—Jayden's sister—were also driving from Kansas. They would stay with his parents at their ranch—about fifty miles away.

~

Rehearsal went much as all rehearsals do. No question to anyone present how happy Jefferson and Martie were. She would have a bouquet of wildflowers for the wedding, as her daughter-in-law Jerilyn did. For the rehearsal, there was one of plastic flowers that Josh had grabbed from somewhere.

Nothing took the place of the rings, just pretend, imagination, dreaming, looking forward to the next day when they would be real. At the end of the rehearsal, the pastor said, "Tomorrow, this would be when I pronounce you man and wife. So, any questions? Do you all feel confident?"

No words from anyone involved, so he continued, "Good. See you all at Eddie's, then here tomorrow for the very special day."

As Pastor Sanders mentioned, the dinner was held at Eddie's Café, which had set aside a special area for the family. Though he would spend the night elsewhere, Jefferson drove Martie home in his SUV. When they got to her house, they sat for a while, holding hands, remembering the rehearsal, practice for tomorrow's wedding.

He asked her to wait while he got out, went around to her door, and helped her out. Their arms went around each other, and there was a kiss before he walked her to her door. After one more kiss, she went inside.

~

It was the day. Jefferson had spent the night with Jerilyn and Josh after taking Martie home. He was so nervous he thought, *It's good I'm here, there's help if I need it.*

Martie was glad to have her daughter to help her get dressed. Nancy and Mitchell had driven in early for that purpose. She brought her dress and would get dressed there also.

~

It was a wonderful, happy day, as all wedding days should be. Many of those in attendance had watched the growing relationship of Martie and Jefferson from their first meeting at a wedding where they were the attendants, then seeing them enjoying dances and loving their time together at other weddings. Living so far apart, but realizing they wanted to see, be with the other, and coordinating circumstances to make it so.

Martie was glad to see her brother and his wife and introduce them to Jefferson. Brent and Mary were glad for the short visit and with Nancy and Mitchell too. Brent said, "We need to plan a get-together, not let so much time pass between visits." The thought was seconded by the rest of them.

When it was time for speeches, tradition was set aside. All of Martie's and Jefferson's children wanted to voice their thoughts. And feeling they had witnessed much of the progress of the romance, the guests were anxious to learn the kids' reactions.

They all expressed similar thoughts about Martie's and Jefferson's courtship. There was surprise, wonder, curiosity, and maybe skepticism. And in the end, there was happiness that their parents had found a new love, and how the family had grown. Their words meant much to the couple.

Someone mentioned they had heard nothing about a honeymoon. Jefferson and Martie were standing hand in hand and smiled at each other, telling anyone who might wonder, "We haven't planned anything specific. For now, being together will be a honeymoon."

There was the dance. The couple had enjoyed those other dances so much, no way would they not include that as part of the day. Afterwards was the toss of the bridal bouquet, caught by an excited young lady from their church.

Confetti had been distributed to the guests and was flung at the couple as they dashed to Jeff's SUV. Only they knew where they were headed, but Kitty had been taken to Josh and Jerilyn's to take care of for a couple of days.

When they were settled in the car, before he started the engine, Jefferson told Martie, "I love you so much. I pray wherever we are, wherever we go in the future, we will be happy and that love continues to grow."

"And I love you and pray the same," Martie said. "I believe God wanted us to have someone that we might love again and used certain circumstances—perhaps weddings—to bring us together."

Anne Edmondson Barbour is a farm girl who grew up in south-west Missouri. At age seventeen, she graduated from high school. Shortly afterward, she got a job in the advertising department of a daily newspaper in the county seat. Though it consisted mostly of secretarial work, occasionally there was the opportunity to write copy for some of the ads. There were other jobs after that, but through the years, she put her writing talent to work in various circumstances, from writing skits for her Cub Scout den, to newsletters for various organizations, to PR for different entities as part of her job. She took a writers' course by mail, but it was not until she was in her eighties that she ventured into writing novels—romances. *To Love Again* is the sixth book in the Love Connections Series. Anne was happily married for almost sixty years, and is now a widow with five children, ten grandchildren, and eight great-grandchildren, with number nine expected this year.